BEFORE YOU FIRE A SHOT...

Thunder Moon gave his companion lessons: first, the mere holding of a rifle; and then its balance in the hands, and how to mark with the eye, before glancing through the sights; and how to find the bull's-eye. How to aim a little low; and then, how to squeeze the trigger with a gradual pressure so that the explosion always would come with a bit of surprise even to the firer. He showed the boy all of these things.

"For," he said, "you know whether your man is dead before the bullet reaches him. You know it by the way you held the gun on the mark."

WARNER BOOKS BY
MAX BRAND

Man From Savage Creek

Trouble Trail

Timbal Gulch Trail

The Sheriff Rides

Valley Vultures

Marbleface

The Return of the Rancher

Bull Hunter

Wild Freedom

Mountain Riders

Slow Joe

Happy Jack

Brothers on the Trail

The Happy Valley

The King Bird Rides

The Long Chance

Mistral

Smiling Charlie

The Rancher's Revenge

The Dude

Silvertip's Roundup

The Man from the Wilderness

Gunfighter's Return

Rider of the High Hill

Way of the Lawless

Storm on the Range

THUNDER MOON'S CHALLENGE

Max Brand

WARNER BOOKS

A Warner Communications Company

Thunder Moon's Challenge is comprised of the following stories, which were originally published in *Western Story Magazine* and written under the name of George Owen Baxter: *Red Wind and Thunder Moon, Thunder Moon-Paleface,* and *Thunder Moon-Squaman.*

WARNER BOOKS EDITION

Copyright 1927 by *Street & Smith Publications, Inc.* **Copyright renewed 1955** by *Dorothy Faust.* **Copyright © 1982** by *Judith Faust, Jane F. Easton and John Frederick Faust.*
All rights reserved.

This Warner Books Edition is published by arrangement with *Dodd, Mead & Company,*
79 Madison Avenue,
New York, N.Y. 10016

Warner Books, Inc.
666 Fifth Avenue
New York, N.Y. 10103

 A Warner Communications Company

Printed in the United States of America

First Warner Books Printing: *June, 1984*

10 9 8 7 6 5 4 3 2 1

THUNDER MOON'S CHALLENGE

PART

ONE

CHAPTER

1

When Walking Horse came to visit the Suhtai band of the Cheyennes, that over which Big Hard Face was the leading chief, it was an event of great importance. Not that such visits were at all rare, as of a warrior passing for a time or even permanently into another of the ten allied bands of the nations, but that Walking Horse was no common brave. Among the Omissis of the Cheyennes he was the very foremost and leading name; he had built up such a fame supported on such hardy achievements in battle that it was almost as though half the power of the Omissis, condensed in the person of one man, had come to sit down among the Suhtais.

His visit, also, was made significant by various details of his conduct. In the first place, though he was absolutely the principal chief among his tribesmen, he came alone, with no following whatever. In the second place, he came among the Suhtai and found there a number of old friends, former associates in battles, grave and celebrated figures. He visited in one tepee and then in another. He talked of the hunt, of the war trails on which he had ridden with them and with others, of the prosperity of the Cheyennes, and of the devilishness of the Pawnees. But never a word did he say of the cause of his visit!

All of this was very singular, of course. The outer world, which has mistaken the shyness of the Indian among strangers for taciturnity, perhaps will feel inclined to say that this essential silence was the nature of the man and of all his peers; but, as a matter of fact, the Indian talks as fast as running water when he is among tried companions. Yet Walking Horse of the Omissis said not a word of his reasons for this visit. For a fortnight he was among them, and still not a word of explanation had been given. And whispers of wonder ran back and forth through the camp!

Then came a band of three well-known warriors from the Omissis. They saw their chief. They proposed to him a promising plan for a raid upon the Sioux; but Walking Horse turned to them a deaf ear. After that, they asked him how long he would be absent from his people; and they received no rejoinder. Further than this, mystified, hurt, and desperate, they drifted here and there among the Suhtai lodges and asked cautiously: What was the purpose that kept their chief so long from home? Affairs of the greatest importance were up for discussion in the councils of the Omissis; why did not their war chief come home?

Of course, the Suhtai had no answer. And the suspense grew greater and greater.

What was the purpose in the mind of this great man? Had his feelings been wounded by some slight received from his followers? Did he contemplate joining himself to the Suhtai permanently? It made the Suhtai chiefs scowl. Not one of them wished to be elbowed from his place by such an addition to the roll of the great ones in the camp; it made the common warriors glad, for many and many a youth yearned to follow such a famous leader.

So a month passed, and then Walking Horse went out from the village to the place where Big Hard Face was watching his great herd of ponies grazing.

Wrapped in their robes, the two chiefs stood side by side and regarded the horses.

"You are rich, December," said the visitor.

December means Big Hard Face, just as November is called Hard Face by the Cheyennes. And as a matter of fact, Big Hard Face was not given that name because he was ugly, but because he was born in the last month of the year.

"I am rich," admitted Big Hard Face, with a grunt of satisfaction.

"But the horses are not big in stature as they are in numbers," went on the Omissis.

"They are greater in heart than in body," replied December. "Look at them again!"

The Omissis made a little pause and pretended to look; but, as a matter of fact, long before this he had examined the herd in the greatest detail and saw that there was not a single weed in the lot. Small they might be, on the whole, but there was not one to whose hardihood and speed a chief of chiefs might not be proud to trust himself and all his fortunes. Surely a rich strain of blood was represented here!

"I have looked," said Walking Horse at last. "They are very good," he admitted.

"They are Comanche horses," said December, concealing his satisfaction as well as he could. "There is not one among them that is not a Comanche."

For of all the tribes that rode upon the plains, the Comanches were famous for the excellence of their mounts. Perhaps it was because, on their many raids into old Mexico, they had seized the cream of the Spanish horses again and again and so purified the strain of their herds; perhaps it was that the desert life of their southern ranges tempered and hardened their horseflesh. At any rate, mounted upon their ponies their stroke was like the stroke of lightning, and if they failed, the hostile tribes could not pursue them in their flight.

"All Comanches! All Comanches!" murmured Walking Horse. "Then you have given a great treasure for so many!"

"I have not given," said December, touching the beadwork that encrusted his robe so richly, "I have not given so much as the value of a single one of these beads."

"They were all taken in war, then?" asked the other, drawing in his breath a little.

"They were taken in war, brother!"

Walking Horse regarded the older man for a moment. Big Hard Face was well advanced in age. His strength had turned heavy upon him but he had not yet withered and grown weak. Yet no one could imagine him swooping down on the agile Comanches in distant raids.

"They are gifts," said the old man in explanation. "All the gifts of Thunder Moon, my son."

"One does not need to be a hawk to see Thunder Moon on the earth," said the Omissis. "And one does not need the ears of an owl to hear his name. Because of him, how many lodges are empty in the camps of the Comanches, and how many of their young wives gash their flesh and cut their hair short and sit in the dust to mourn! But if I had a wish to buy from you fifty of these horses of the Comanches, what price would you place upon them all, brother?"

December gathered his robe a little closer about him and cast a glance brighter than fire at his companion; the lust of the trader was hot in his soul.

"That is a thing to consider," said he.

"A horse is a horse," replied the Omissis, "and a woman is no more than a woman. These things all have their price!"

"Would you ask an eagle for the value of his wings?" asked Big Hard Face, a most cunning bargainer. "If I wish to send out the best of my young men on a great raid, when they must fly far and fast, I lead out these horses of mine. I place the young warriors on their backs. It is then as though I had placed them on the back of the wind. They ride out. They are so fast that their enemies cannot see them in midday. They strike. They count a hundred coups. And then they return to my village and before their faces a great cloud of dust rolls up to the heart of the sky. It is raised by the hooves of the horses they drive back to me."

He waved his hand again toward his herd of horses.

"And now you ask me," said he, "at what price I will be willing to sell fifty of these?"

"Horses are good," replied the Omissis, taking the time-honored track of all traders making a bargain, "but so are rich robes covered with beads, and robes painted by cunning hands; new strong guns are good, and so are much powder and lead, and keen knives, and sugar, and coffee!"

Big Hard Face grinned and showed two or three large fangs in the black shapeless slit of his mouth.

"They are good," said he, "sugar is good!"

He licked his lips, and drew in a great breath.

"Pounds and pounds of sugar," said the Omissis cleverly, "and knives, guns, robes. It is only necessary to name the amount. You are rich, December. Neither am I a poor man."

"When a man stands on a cliff," said Big Hard Face, "one step is life, and one is death. There is no need for hurry. Let us go back to my lodge and speak with Thunder Moon."

Back toward the village they strolled. The wild heat of midday was over. The shadows were reaching toward the east. And from the river the shouts of the playing and swimming boys and young men rose into the air, echoing hollow from the face of the water. Girls were coming in with bundles of firewood broken or cut in the brush. Women were carrying up water. And the smoke was going up from the lodges.

At the entrance to the town, they passed a burly Indian clad in a robe of great price, wearing a strange headdress, which was the scalp of a wolf, mounted with all the terribly grinning teeth. Beneath that uncouth gear there showed a thoughtful, meditative face. He was passing with his eyes upon the ground, but seeing Big Hard Face, he started and raised his hand.

"How!"

"How!" said December, and went on.

"I still wait!" said the man of the wolf's head.

December answered nothing, but went rather more hurriedly on his way.

"Tell me, brother," said the Omissis, who had listened with much curiosity to this brief exchange, "was not that Spotted Bull, the chief among the medicine men of the Suhtai?"

"May he die without a scalp!" exclaimed Big Hard Face.

"May he die as naked as when he was born and the Pawnee wolves count coup on him three times. Why should he fix his teeth in a child of my tepee?"

"Ha!" murmured Walking Horse. "Then he is not a friend to Thunder Moon?"

Big Hard Face sighed, but, as though the matter were too great for words, he said no more of it, and the Omissis did not press the point. So they came to the lodge of Big Hard Face and passed inside. But Big Hard Face, as he passed in through the flap, uttered a little exclamation of disgust and displeasure. For squatting in the middle of the tepee with a flashing scraper in his hand, the son of the chief was hard at work preparing a small buffalo hide.

"Woman's work!" snorted December. "Thunder Moon, do you forget that you are a man?"

CHAPTER

2

Thunder Moon shrugged his broad shoulders and did not turn his head.

"White Crow is old and tired," said he. "Besides, who would sit by the fire all day and make his lungs ache with smoke, or tell stories until the tongue tires?"

And, saying this, he continued to work with the flashing tool, which was a shoulderblade, shaped for the grip of the hands. There was no vestige of clothing on him except for moccasins on his feet, a breech clout, and a narrow band that held back from his face the long shower of black hair that fell glistening over his shoulders and down his back almost to the hips. Now, as he worked with the scraping bone, one could see why no man among all the tall Cheyennes dared to exchange cuffs with him, or wrestle with him hand to hand on equal terms; for, though his arms were not actually massive, they were alive with long, twisting tangles of muscle that swept without a break from shoulder to wrist, and the power across his shoulders knotted and leaped like so many hands being clenched hard beneath the skin.

Walking Horse took curious note of this figure. For though he had been many days among the Suhtai, still he had not had great opportunity for observing Thunder Moon. To the feasts, Thunder Moon went not. And when the circle formed and the coup stick was passed. Thunder Moon would rise and stride from a tepee; neither did he go where the old men talked in the evening.

"Thunder Moon!" exclaimed the old chief in a tone of command.

The young man turned and stood up. Seeing a guest, he greeted him gravely, flushing a little, and threw a robe about his great shoulders. Big Hard Face was terribly displeased, but he swallowed his anger a little. He merely said, "How can a man's work be done by a woman? Or a woman's work by a man?"

"Father," replied Thunder Moon, "tell me this: When a man strikes in a battle, should his hand be heavy or light?"

"That is a child's question," answered the chief.

"Very well," said Thunder Moon, "does the hand grow strong holding a pipe or dipping into the meat pot?"

"It is always like this," said Big Hard Face gloomily, turning to the Omissis. "There is no corner so narrow that he cannot talk his way out of it! There are more words and ways to his tongue than there are buffalo and their trails on the open plains! Now hear me, Thunder Moon. Walking Horse wishes to know the price of fifty of your horses. He is a guest. He is a famous man. Therefore we wish to make his a small price—consider it, Thunder Moon!"

And he made a little private sign to his son, which, in a white man, might well have been replaced by a wink.

Thunder Moon considered. His two elders were seated. He remained standing, and with the butt of a battle spear he prodded at the earth.

"We do not wish to lose so many horses," said he. "But our guest is a famous man. Take fifty from our herd. You need them for the warpath, I suppose? Take them, send out your young men on their backs. If some die on the trail, it is no matter. When you return, keep ten of the best for yourself, and send back the remainder to me. I have spoken."

It seemed as though Big Hard Face would choke, during the latter part of this short speech. His color changed, his eyes started from his scarred, horribly deformed face. But still he dared not say no. It was beneath the dignity of any brave to deny a gift, once proffered, but he writhed to and fro on his couch and hurriedly caught up a pipe that smoke might allay his injured feelings.

As for Walking Horse, no doubt he was familiar with the impulsive generosity of his race, but this was a kingly magnificence that was quite beyond his comprehension. His eyes burned for a moment, and, to mask that greedy fire, he glanced down to the ground. He cleared his throat once or twice and then he began to make a speech. He declared, in many magnificent words, that he would be ashamed to ask a price and then get horses for nothing. One horse he would accept, partly because the Comanche strain was so glorious, but partly because every horse that Thunder Moon had taken from the enemy was a reminder to every Cheyenne of the glory of the taker. That glory grew every day. According to Walking Horse, as he warmed to his work, the whole nation of the Pawnees shuddered in their lodges when they so much as thought of Thunder Moon, and the Comanches hushed the cries of their children with his dreadful name. Accordingly, he, Walking Horse, would accept one pony, the meanest of the herd, as a souvenir of the great man. But, in the meantime, he persisted and begged Thunder Moon to name the price of fifty horses.

Under this shower of praise Thunder Moon at first stood straight; then winced; turned a bright red, which the paleness of his face made more pronounced, and finally seemed to look for an avenue of escape.

At last he said, with a bluntness of which no other Cheyenne, assuredly, would have been guilty, "Your many words make me unhappy. Take whatever horse you please. But great praise means great blame."

He turned to his father, and bade Big Hard Face settle the terms if a price were to be made.

Big Hard Face could wait no longer.

"You see," said he, "that we do not wish to sell. The

heart of Thunder Moon is like a rain cloud. It would dissolve in giving! But since you will not take the gifts he offers,'' went on the chief hurriedly, ''then I shall tell you a cheap price for such horses as run in our herd. One hundred good rifles, and ten of the small guns that have six voices.'' He indicated a revolver that hung from the post at the foot of Thunder Moon's couch. ''Also, much lead and powder, and ten good knives with edges that will not turn. Furthermore, we need some good painted robes, and a suit covered with beads. The Omissis women make many of them. If you will do these things, then you may be sure that you shall have the fifty horses.''

Walking Horse considered these demands with blinking eyes and a shudder.

''Brother,'' he said sadly, ''you ask for enough guns to arm a whole tribe!''

''The Omissis are rich,'' said Big Hard Face coldly, ''and all men know that Walking Horse is the richest of his tribe. His horses make the earth tremble as they gallop together. Two tall and broad tepees cannot hold the mass of his saddles and guns and beaded clothes and knives and beads and other treasures.''

''Ah, brother,'' murmured the visitor, ''rumor is full of lies! I am not so rich.''

He looked appealingly at them, in turn. Big Hard Face endured that appeal with an unmoved countenance, but Thunder Moon frowned at the ground and bit his lip. It was plain that his father's bargaining had shamed him.

''However,'' said the Omissis suddenly, ''if I am not so rich, neither am I poor. You shall have everything as you ask. But in return, I shall want something more than just the fifty horses.''

''Speak,'' said Big Hard Face, his eyes narrowing to shrewdness again. And still there was a faraway light in them, as though already his glance were caressing the heap of weapons for which he had bargained.

''It is a small thing,'' said the other. ''In my tepees there is a thing that I wish to give to Thunder Moon, to be taken into his lodge and cherished. Let Thunder Moon give me his promise that he will accept it; then I shall go to make the long journey to the fort of the white man and bring back all that your hearts desire!''

"You are kind," said Big Hard Face instantly, "and my son accepts your kindness."

"No," put in Thunder Moon, "I have no need of gifts that I do not know. I have a horse to ride, a gun to shoot, and a spear to stab with. What more does a Cheyenne ask of the Sky People?''

"Boy," said his father, "you speak like a fool; you shame me before Walking Horse. Tell him at once that whatever he brings, you will take it and keep it well to honor him!''

Thunder Moon looked narrowly at the Omissis, leaning forward a little and seeming to probe the very soul of the stranger.

"It is well," said he finally. "My father commands me. I give my word to Walking Horse!''

There had been a great tension in the expression of the Omissis up to this time. Now it was as though a burden had been cast from his mind. He stood up, and making some remark about the distance of the journey that he had to perform, he left the tepee almost at once, and five minutes later he had departed from the camp of the Suhtai.

He left a gloomy scene behind him, where Thunder Moon stared at his foster father.

"There was more wealth put in our hands," said Big Hard Face, "than any Suhtai ever has seen in one heap before and been able to call his own. And you would have thrown it away! Thunder Moon, you are a child, and you grow no older with the years!''

"Tell me," said Thunder Moon, "has not Walking Horse acted like a fool, to accept your price without bargaining?''

Big Hard Face smiled with the greatest satisfaction.

"Wisdom is richer than wealth, and cunning thoughts are turned into strong horses," said he.

"And yet," said Thunder Moon, "Walking Horse is not a fool, but a wise chief, and a ruler over chiefs, and a rich man as well.''

Big Hard Face was quite silent, frowning.

"And you may be sure," said the younger man, "that whatever he gives to us will be a thing worse than poison to him."

"Still you have many words," said Big Hard Face. "But words are not medicine. If there is poison in his tepee, would he not throw it away?"

"You will see," said Thunder Moon in reply. "Unless Walking Horse is a fool, I know that he came to us not to buy horses, but to make us take this precious gift. When we receive it, may the Sky People give us strength and wisdom!"

CHAPTER

3

Three important events kept the mission of Walking Horse and his expected return well in the background during the following weeks. In the first place, the tribe moved camp. In the second place, Spotted Bull fell out with Big Hard Face and Thunder Moon. In the third place, Falling Stone made the first of his famous excursions into Cheyenne territory and crossed swords with Thunder Moon.

As for the camp removal, it was no more important than such events usually were, but it called for the making of medicine; and the making of the medicine brought Spotted Bull to the lodge of Big Hard Face. There they sat talking amicably, until the medicine man turned the conversation into other channels.

"I have waited for three months," said the medicine man, "and still Thunder Moon keeps far from me. I never see him in my tepee. On the walls of my lodge hang suits of rich beadwork, and I have painted robes and knives and guns given to me by the braves of the Suhtai, but I have nothing from the hand of Thunder Moon."

December made a slight grimace.

"My son shall remember you," said he. "Go home, and you will find three horses at your tepee. They will let you know that Thunder Moon is your friend."

"A gift that is asked for is meat that chokes the gullet," said the medicine man grimly. "It is not for added riches that I sorrow, but it is because the young men come to me and say, 'From whom did these good things come?' Then I name the givers. Behold, all the brave men of our tribe are then named and many famous men from among all of the Cheyennes whose children and wives I have healed, from whose fortunes I have taken curses, and whose guns I have given power on the warpath! But at last I must stop. They look at me in wonder. They say, 'What is the gift of our greatest warrior; our hero with the heart of a charging bull; our wisest councilor, who has the strongest hand and who keeps the richest tepee? What is the gift of Thunder Moon?' Then I am silent, I hang my head, and men go away wondering."

Spotted Bull had retained his calm, but only through a considerable effort, and now he was breathing hard. He could hardly compel himself to take the pipe that December, filled with trouble, passed to him.

"Consider the soul of a young man," said Big Hard Face. "It is like the wind that roves through the sky. It blows here and it blows there, not because one-quarter of the heaven is better than another, but because it has an idle way!"

The medicine man snorted as he blew out smoke to the earth and smoke to the sky.

"Tell me this," he answered, "of the foolish youths of our tribe, who are like colts, throwing up their heels and running from grass to water and from water to grass. But Thunder Moon has a mind that thinks, and when he looks into the face of a man, he is like one who reads the sign of a trail. For all that he does he has a good reason, even though his reasons are not anything like the reasons of the rest of the Suhtai!"

The anger of Spotted Bull was growing. His host feebly fumbled here and there in his wits, but he could think of nothing that might appease his guest.

Said Spotted Bull in continuation, "Is my medicine bad? What else has given fortune to Big Hard Face? What has turned the weapons of his enemies away from his breast when he rode to war? But now there is a greater medicine in his tepee, men say!''

And with a malignant smile, he pointed to a glittering thing made of yellow metal, which hung from the central pole of the tepee, shaped roughly and rudely into the semblance of a human arm.

December looked in the same direction. There was much respect in his voice as he said, ''That is a piece of the Yellow Man, the greatest medicine that the Comanches owned. Has not their luck left them since Thunder Moon carried their medicine away from them? Have they not run from before the faces of the Suhtai? And has not Thunder Moon prospered in all things because of that medicine, brother?''

A deep, guttural exclamation from Spotted Bull showed December that he had touched a most tender point.

''I know it!'' said the medicine man. ''That was the knowledge that the spirits whispered to me when they said that an enemy was lodged in the tepee of December. The Yellow Man has always done mischief to the Cheyennes. When he was with the Comanches he turned their bullets into the hearts of our warriors. Now he only can turn Suhtai against Suhtai. But always he is the enemy of my tribe! Throw away that cursed token, brother. Give it to me. Let me purify it. Let me hang it in my tent. I shall accept the danger that comes out of it!''

He rose from his place, touched the symbol, weighed it in his hand.

''Yes,'' he said. ''I shall take it from you!''

''Brother,'' said the chief in a dry voice, ''take heed for yourself. Do not take it. My son would be angry!''

''The anger of a man,'' replied Spotted Bull, ''is nothing to me. Neither yours nor your son's. I have to do with such great spirits, December, that if I call them now, they would leap down out of the sky and turn you and all that is in your tepee into mist, so that the people who passed would see no more than a big smoke going upward from this pipe of mine!''

He said it solemnly, and December, listening with starting eyes, shuddered and sighed.

"But," went on the medicine man, who saw that he had made a point, "I am your friend, and I wish to be the friend of Thunder Moon. I have been his friend all these days, without gift or without kindness from him. I have prayed for his success on the warpath. I have offered up sacrifice. I have taken out the sacred medicine pipes for his sake! But I have no reward. I have not gone among the people and said to them in times of misfortune, 'You are hungry and cold, but may that not be because you keep in your midst a man who makes strange medicine? A man who speaks with the tongue of a Suhtai, but whose heart is not the heart of a Suhtai.'"

He paused. Big Hard Face sat up stiffly.

"What lying spirit has told you that his spirit is not the spirit of a Suhtai? Is he not my son?"

The medicine man could not restrain a grin of triumph and malice.

"Is your skin the color of my skin?" he said.

"That is true."

"And we are Suhtai, brother. But the skin of Thunder Moon is the pale skin of a white man! He is not your son. He is a stranger. His heart is a stranger's heart!"

The eyes of Big Hard Face flickered from side to side. If ever danger were written visibly on the face of a man, it was written on the face of December.

"This is not good talking," he said huskily. "Brother, beware!"

"I remember," said Spotted Bull, "when you left the camp—it was many years ago—and you were gone many, many days. When you came back, you had the child with you. You took him into your tepee. You got him a Suhtai name. He was a member of the tribe. But he is a white man. He is not one of us. How would it be, December, if I told these things to Thunder Moon himself?"

"If," replied Big Hard Face ominously, "you separate a father from a son, because of the wrong words your spirits have told you . . ."

He could not say anything more. His eyes, however, were fire.

And the medicine man continued smoothly, "I have no wish to make trouble. That is for the medicine of the Yellow Man, yonder, to do. But I work against him. I try to keep peace in our city. I make our young warriors like brothers on the trail. Only—I tell you again: Let Thunder Moon come to me. Let him open his heart to me like a child to a father. All still may be well between us. All still may be well!"

Having said this, he got up at once and left the tepee, gathering his dignity about him like a robe, and left December behind him lost in gloomy reflections.

When Thunder Moon came in from the hunt—with three horses loaded with antelope meat, for when did he return empty-handed?—then the old chief sent White Crow away from the lodge and sat down before the blood of the hunt was washed from his hands. Not all of the conversation with Spotted Bull was repeated, but enough was said to explain that the tepee and all in it, especially Thunder Moon, were in danger of the terrible wrath of the medicine man. Their bodies might be twisted with deformities. Their horses might be stolen. Their arms might grow powerless. The bullets of the enemy might be turned into their hearts, their scalps hung at the belt of Pawnee warriors, and their souls left to wander miserably up and down the winds of the earth until, at last, they dwindled, grew thin, and disappeared forever!

When the young man had heard it, he answered gravely, "Father, you are old and you are wise. You know how to speak before the council. You understand how to hunt the buffalo. You know many things, and every day I sit at your knee like a child and drink in your words and your wisdom. But as for Spotted Bull, and as for all the doctors of our tribe and of all other tribes, and the medicine that they make, I think they are no more than scoundrels or fools, and that their medicine is folly! I will not have it!"

Big Hard Face hastily threw sweet grass on the fire and went through the motions of bathing himself in the purifying smoke. He did the same for his son.

"Do not speak like this," he complained. "Words may be

more dangerous than Pawnee bullets. It is not much to go to
the tepee of Spotted Bull and say that you are his friend! It
will cost you nothing!''

"It will cost me a lie," said Thunder Moon.

"It will cost you only a word."

"Look!" said the youth. "Now, I am as free as any man
could wish to be. I go where I will over the prairie. I pass in
and I pass out from the village, and I am my own master,
except when you command me, and you are the chief of our
tribe. I do not even belong to any of the soldier bands. No
man can compel me to do one thing if I choose to do another.
But now you want me to make a slave of my mind to Spotted
Bull. I shall not be his slave. I laugh at him, and if he crosses
me, I shall laugh in his face, and beat him into his tepee. He
is a villain and a fool. You want to make me worse than a
squaw; worse than the stupid white men, who are not able to
live under the sky, and who have to have roofs over their
heads, making their heaven out of wood. No, father, I must
be free. All medicine is foolishness."

"Do you never pray?" asked the old man, angry but
baffled.

"Yes," said Thunder Moon. "I pray to the Sky People.
They send a shining cloud across the face of the heavens. I
know that they have heard my prayer. It always has been so
since I was a boy. I shall go out and ask them now if I have
been wrong!"

CHAPTER

4

Beyond the village, seated on his horse on the top of a hill, Thunder Moon looked up to the sky and raised his hands. So much was seen by Big Hard Face. For an entire half hour the young man remained in that position, though the sun must almost have blinded his eyes. And then, forming suddenly in the middle of the sky, a cloud of a dazzling whiteness appeared and blew softly down toward the northern horizon.

Big Hard Face watched no longer from the distance, but went hastily back to his tepee, his mind revolving many doubts. Of the success of his foster child in war the whole tribe could bear witness. Of the wisdom of Thunder Moon, all the council of the old men and the heroes could speak, also. For what plan of war was considered unless Thunder Moon were in the camp to give his advice? And so it had been from the days of his youth, and most particularly since that famous expedition against the Comanches that had brought back the arm of the Yellow Man from the southern riders. Yet there were gaps in the strength of Thunder Moon, and no man was so acutely aware of them as December. There had been a

21

time when his life had been turned to a hell of misery. In those days the croaking voice of White Crow, his aunt and the only woman of his tepee, continually pointed out the weakness of the foster child. And, as she had said in those days, Thunder Moon never was one to endure pain like a brave Indian; even as a young man, sudden agony could wring a cry from his lips. And when the other young braves drew their belts tighter and endured famine on the trail, Thunder Moon grew faint; just as he grew faint if the race were long on foot. Neither had he even the craft of a ten-year-old boy in reading the signs of the war trail; and his eyes and his ears seemed to be half blinded or deafened. In all these matters he was lacking, and great matters they were. But he had worse faults and follies. He took no joy in slaying an enemy from ambush, but, like a madman, he loved the battle only when he endured a peril in order to inflict an injury. And, in the middle of a battle, had he not been known, like a witless creature, to go insane with battle passion and charge straight through the line of the enemy, shooting to the right and to the left? These indeed were things to be wondered at, but greater stupidity remained behind. To any sensible Plains Indian, there were three necessary parts to battle: One was the counting of the coup, one was the slaying of the foe, one was the taking of his scalp. And their importance was, first, the counting of the coup; second, the taking of the scalp; and, last of all, the actual slaying of the foeman. Yet with Thunder Moon, these matters were reversed. He would not take a scalp and he would not have his clothes trimmed with scalp locks, or hang them from the bridle of his horse, for he declared that they were disgusting emblems. And for the counting of coup, he scorned the ceremony and announced that it had no meaning to touch the body of an enemy. But to kill—ah, that was a different matter! Never had there been a Cheyenne in the remembrance of old December to match this adroit hunter of the Pawnee and the Comanche! Never had there been another to equal his list of the slain. And in battle, the charge of Thunder Moon was like the charge of an entire squadron! The foe could not stand against him!

So he had virtues to balance against his faults. No Indian

could handle a rifle with such remorseless skill; few even possessed the new small revolvers that were so deadly in the possession of Thunder Moon. If even the boys could outlast him in a long run, not the most brilliant athlete could escape from him in a short sprint; just as the mountain lion overtakes the wolf although it cannot run all day across the plains. So, too, he had such wisdom in council as made the old men wonder, and he seemed able to read the minds of friends and foes. And the same iron that seemed to nerve his hand for an encounter and make it resistless was in his wits also.

He was so different from the rest of the tribesmen that he never could become a chief. He was so necessary to them that they could not imagine the Suhtai without his help! And because of him, old December remained in his lofty position as leader of the tribe! But now, as December revolved the words of the medicine man again and again, he wondered if it were not true that not only the skin but the soul of his foster child was white. And, if that were the case, might he not, on a day, return to his people?

Big Hard Face drew his robe about his face. There he sat, shrouded in darkness, when his son returned and announced in a quiet, cheerful voice that all was well; the Sky People approved of what he had said and done concerning Spotted Bull, for they had sent him a visible sign not many moments before!

Big Hard Face returned no answer. For his soul was sore! And during the days that followed, he waited for the danger to strike at him from the hand of the medicine man.

Cunning to argue with his foster son he lacked. And all he could do was to endure, and hope for the best. The croaking voice of White Crow did not help him. Time could wither her, but it could not take the strength from her sinewy arm, or the deathless malice from her tongue. She had heard enough of the trouble between Thunder Moon and the medicine man, and her dry dusty voice rattled out prophecies of evil for long time to come!

But, before any blow was struck by Spotted Bull, who seemed to be waiting with an admirable patience for some approach from Thunder Moon, a blow of another sort struck

the entire village. It was the first raid of Falling Stone, a
rising young brave among the Pawnees. Now, in the flower of
his youth, he had reached such consideration among his
tribesmen that they had sent him out with a large body of
warriors. He stole up close to the Suhtai camp, and just with
the setting of the sun he rushed his horsemen up from the
hollow by the river. Half the entire horse herd was swept
away by that charge; and leading his warriors on into the
outskirts of the village, Falling Stone and they rode down,
slew, and counted coup upon more than twenty people,
mostly women and children. But a death is a death, and a
coup is a coup, and all are equally honorable, all equally
swell the fame of an Indian.

Then, behind the stampeded horses, Falling Stone rushed
away across the prairie, having dealt the Cheyennes such a
blow as they had not received in years from their traditional
enemies. The vengeance party was assembled at once, all the
best and the bravest of the young men; and, as a matter of
course, Thunder Moon was there to lead them. There was
only a hasty consultation with Spotted Bull, but in that brief
moment he struck his blow. He came out in his full medicine
regalia, a nightmare figure, and he chanted to the excited
listeners a pretended revelation from the spirits, bidding the
Suhtai no longer to follow the leadership of Thunder Moon—
certainly not until he had been purified in the eyes of the Sky
People for his sins!

At such a time as this, while a war party was actually
arming in haste, there was no question of doubting the advice
of the inspired prophet. With the tried and trusted hero,
Standing Bear, to lead them, the war party rushed away on
the trail of the Pawnees; but Thunder Moon remained for a
little behind them.

He sat his horse before Spotted Bull; women, and children,
and old men surrounded them.

"Spotted Bull," said he, "has my good fortune left me?"

"Alas, my son," said the medicine man, "what your sins
have been, you know as well as I. The spirits tell me; your
heart tells you what you have done that is wrong."

"But tell me, Spotted Bull. Am I to bring back none of the

stolen horses, and are no Pawnees to fall under my rifle?" asked the youth.

"I have said it," answered Spotted Bull, gathering his robe about him. "It is only a fool who asks a man to repeat a thing that he has said once!"

Behind him, his uncle and his young nephew had guns in hand, ready to defend him in case Thunder Moon's proverbially heavy hand threatened to descend on Spotted Bull; but the other merely laughed, sitting at ease on the back of one of his Comanche ponies, with a led horse beside him.

"I go on that trail," said he. "When I come back, I shall let the people see that Spotted Bull is a liar and a fool!"

And he rode away into the night, leaving consternation behind him. As for old December, he was lost in bewilderment and woe. What would be the outcome of this duel between his foster child and the most powerful medicine man in the tribe he could not guess. But he gravely doubted. Every Suhtai prejudice would be on the side of Spotted Bull.

And, in fact, no sooner had the warrior departed than Spotted Bull began to rouse sentiment against Thunder Moon— openly and in private he talked. The old men listened. The children gabbled the news about the village; the women could talk of nothing else. All that could be said against Thunder Moon was brought forth now—how as a boy he had failed in the test of courage by which the Cheyennes pass from boyhood to manhood and become worthy of the war trail. So that, indeed, he could hardly be called a warrior at all! And how pain frightened him! And how he failed in his reverence to the spirits and offered them no sacrifice! And how, even in battle, he would count no coups, he would take no scalps!

"Because he dares not!" said the medicine man. "He has no medicine except the medicine that he stole from the Comanches, and that is poison for a true Cheyenne. But this man has a white skin. He has a white heart. Let him go back to his own people!"

These words were reported in due course to old December. If he had not heard them from rumor, he would have heard them from White Crow, as she worked in the tepee.

"Woman," thundered the chief in a fury, at last, "do you hate Thunder Moon?"

She raised her head and looked at him with bright, beady eyes.

"I am a Cheyenne!" said she.

"Is that an answer?" cried December. "Am I not a Cheyenne, also?"

"I am a Cheyenne, and a Suhtai!" said she.

Big Hard Face glared at her evilly for another moment, and then he turned and rushed from the lodge into the darkness that waited for him outside—darkness of the night, and darkness of his troubled spirit.

CHAPTER

5

For a whole day the eager horsemen of the Suhtai rushed across the plains of the hot trail of Falling Stone and the Pawnees; and toward dusk of the second day they came to a shallow stream and began to ford it in haste. Nearly half of them were across when the ground before them quivered and the air was stirred by the rapid drumming of many hooves, as over the brow of the farther slope Falling Stone with all his warriors banded behind him drove down upon the Cheyennes. The Suhtai, disordered, tired from the long march, straggling here and there, or heaped close together, just as they had come out of the ford, did not think of resistance for a moment. They turned to flee, and as they fled, the bullets and the showered arrows of the Pawnees dealt death among them, and the reaching spears stabbed them in the back. Right on into the water, which foamed with blood and with tramplings, the Pawnees charged; and then, at a shrill command from their leader, they swerved away suddenly back to the bank and from the cover of the shrubbery that lined the shore, all lying prostrate and taking secure aim, they pelted the yelling Cheyennes with bullets and with arrows again.

The Cheyennes had received a dreadful check; fifty of their best and bravest lay dead, scalped, unburied behind them; the bodies plundered, the sacred medicine bags gone, and the corpses flung into the river, where they were rolled and tumbled and battered and hurried far away. Plainly, the medicine that accompanied the Suhtai upon this expedition was of little strength, and therefore the band turned sadly back toward the distant village. And even then, Falling Stone would not have done, but with a dozen of his best rifles he hung on the rear of the defeated host and quickly bagged a round half dozen laggards.

When had there been such another day as this for the Pawnees? When such another for the Suhtai band? On the farther shore of the river, secure beyond its waters, Falling Stone pitched his camp at last and prepared to give his men a full day of rest and rejoicing and feasting before they continued the march. For all his braves had counted at least one brave.

From the woods that crowned the slope, Falling Stone had trees cut and dragged down whole to the edge of the water. There the great fire was lighted, and around it smaller camp fires glimmered here and there, surrounded by warriors cooking, but the feasting was interrupted by the revel of the rejoicing. All those Pawnees were mad with delight, and they sent their shouts beating up against the night sky.

They were not unheard. In the edge of the trees a solitary warrior looked down on the flames of the fires and the figures of the dancers, leaping up black and tall; he listened to the yells of triumph, and his soul swelled high.

Stretched along the lower branch of a tree, his horse picketed well behind him in the wood, Thunder Moon stared at the Pawnees and trembled with indignation, like a hungry wolf watching in the distance the banqueting of many coyotes, too numerous to be attacked even by his superior might of tooth and shoulder.

He did not have the patience of an Indian; but he had a patience that any white man could have admired, as he lay there hour after hour, and saw the fires diminish, heard the cries of joy grow fewer, and the screech of horn and whistle die out. Glutted with victory and with boasting, the Pawnees fell asleep. Only here and there a few hardy enthusiasts, chiefly very young men who had not counted a coup before, continued the dancing and the merrymaking. Now, a tall brave hurried up the slope, ax in hand, to bring back wood, for the main fire. The spirit of the dance still was upon him, and as he went, he leaped up and down, and his whoop went thrilling behind him. Straight under the tree of Thunder Moon he passed. Down upon him dropped a shadow; the Pawnee fell without a sound, and there was the heavy, hollow sound of a knife driven home by a strong hand. His medicine bag passed into the possession of the victor, and Thunder Moon stood up and laughed down at the noise of the celebration. He laughed silently, for now he could turn back to the far-off village. He had done his deed, counted his coup, and he could return and tell his disheartened people that Spotted Bull was a liar and a fool, who made medicine without strength, and who could not give strength to his friends, nor unnerve his enemies. The proof was the medicine bag of this fallen Pawnee.

Yet suppose Spotted Bull declared that the bag must have been picked up from where it lay forgotten on the battlefield?

Thunder Moon lingered on the edge of the woods and passed his tongue across his dry lips. He was athirst with a burning of the soul, which cried out for the blood of Pawnees—and there they were spread out before him, enough to feast even his vengeance! Ah, those wolves of the plains!

Now the moon rose, hanging a bright, golden disk in the east, and he took it as a token. He went back to the place where his horse was left and found there his spear, plunged into the ground, and his shield hanging from it. Both these he took and returned with them to the forest's edge, and then advanced into the open a few steps and held up shield and spear to the rising moon. It was a dream shield of wonderful power, made in the old days by a forefather of Young Hawk, and bequeathed by him to Thunder Moon when the brave died. No bullet struck the warrior who carried that shield in

battle! It was round, made of thickened bull's hide covered
with well-dressed antelope skin. Eagle feathers hung from it,
to signify the flight and the power of the king of the sky; and
it was painted with the mysterious form of the crescent moon,
the horns turned upward, and there were four spots, to
represent the four winds of heaven.

This shield, and the long lance, Thunder Moon raised to
the moon which now floated in the black bowl of the sky, to
the zenith, and to the west. But last, he presented it straight
to the moon again and made this prayer aloud:

"White Spirit, look down on me and see me standing here.
I am not a stranger to you; my name was taken from your
brother, who looks through the thunder clouds; and your
image is painted on this magic shield, which has covered me
in battle so that the arrows, the spears, the bullets, the knives
of all my enemies cannot harm me in war. The Sioux, the
Comanches, the Crows, the Blackfeet, and the Pawnees know
this shield and they know me who carry it. I am Thunder
Moon. No man among the Cheyennes is so strong as I. No
man has killed so many enemies. Wherever the plains stretch
from the north to the south and from the great river into the
western mountains, I am known and I am feared. But I know
that it is not my strength that conquers but the strength of the
Sky People, and chiefly yours. If ever I have sacrificed to you
swift horses, and whole buffalo, and beaded suits, and weapons, and painted robes, hear me now! The Pawnee wolves lie
by the river, and their bellies are filled with meat; but their
brains are more filled with victory over my people who have
been fools and trusted to the medicine of a cheat instead of
worshiping the Sky People. Now, I stand under your white
face and wait and watch for a sign to tell me whether I may
safely go down among them and come back again, having
done things they will remember. Speak to me, Spirit!"

Lance and shield extended above his head stiffly, at arm's
length, face raised, Thunder Moon waited through long
minutes. He seemed to have turned to iron, to be incapable of
weariness.

At last he said in a low voice, "My arms fall from my
shoulders; my head swims; speak to me quickly!"

And instantly, as though this message had been heard, a wisp of cloud blew across the disk in the sky, not darkening it, but rather absorbing the light and hanging for a moment like a shining scarf before it vanished.

Thunder Moon drew in a great breath; then, with an effort, he stilled the shout of triumph that trembled in his throat. He turned and hastened back to his horse, where he drove the lance into the ground again, hung the sacred shield reverently upon it—for these weapons would be useless in the work that he intended—and then started straight down the slope for the camp. Even his rifle he had not brought with him, but in the front of his belt was his knife, long-bladed, heavy and strong as a short sword. With a stroke of that knife he had severed the spinal cord of a running buffalo. He carried, moreover, a heavy Colt revolver in a sheath of antelope skin against his thigh, fastened low down, so that it was ready for the quick and practiced touch of his fingers. So equipped, he felt that he could give death to seven Pawnees before he died in turn, if the worst came to the worst. But the moon shone behind him, and he did not fear the brightness of its light. Rather, it was a heavenly companion that filled his heart with courage. For had he not prayed and had not his prayer been answered?

So he went down the slope hastily. A true Indian of the plains would have moved with less than half his noise, especially through the tall, dried grasses that covered the slope, but his heart was armed with enchanted power, and he was not afraid!

He came up to the camp not crawling, but upright, like a man who feels his destiny upon him. Just below the camp was a deep little swale, and as he stepped into it, a form rose before him and held a rifle at his breast.

"What is your name, brother?" asked the Pawnee. "Have you gone out to give thanks to the night for your dead men?"

"Yes," said Thunder Moon in the Pawnee tongue, which he had learned perfectly from prisoners, "and you are the second man!"

And as he spoke, the knife was conjured into his hand and driven into the heart of the warrior. The latter gave a gasping, half-stifled groan. And Thunder Moon, catching the body to keep it from crashing down among the rattling grasses, listened breathlessly. Apparently, the groan had not been heard in the Pawnee camp. Only the wind whispered guiltily among the long grasses and, far off, a horse neighed from the opposite side of the sleeping camp.

Then Thunder Moon, his heart swelling with gratitude and joy, stood erect. He held the limp body of the Pawnee up to the moon, and whispered, "This death, and the medicine bag of this warrior, I sacrifice to you, white face!"

Then he laid the body softly in the grass, took the medicine bag from about its neck, and walked confidently on into the midst of his enemies.

CHAPTER

6

Most in that camp were sleeping, exhausted by their riding, their battle, and their rejoicings; but many still were awake, and Thunder Moon passed within a dozen strides of some of them. However, their eyes were partly blinded by the brightness of their camp fires, and partly their suspicions were blinded and could not quite waken at the sight of this tall, naked warrior, striding through the camp.

The prairie sun had bronzed the body of Thunder Moon to a darkness almost as coppery as the color of the true Indian; and, by the moonlight, there was nothing to betray him except the length of his hair, which flowed far, after the fashion of the Cheyennes. However, he had disguised himself sufficiently in this particular by catching up and putting on one of those wolfish headdresses of which the Pawnees were so fond.

He went straight to the center of the camp where the chiefs should be found. And now he told himself that if he could know the face and form of the leader of this brilliant war party he could strike a blow at the Pawnees that, almost at a single stroke, would overbalance the whole work of this expedition. But he looked down upon an array of scattered warriors all in the prime of life, magnificent men, wrapped in buffalo robes; all fit to lead such an expedition, as he thought.

Their lances were fixed in the ground. Their shields hung upon them. They seemed to Thunder Moon like silent guardians of the sleepers. And, passing man after man, his lips twitched and his fingers tingled for his weapon. How simple it would be to lean and with a stroke of the knife send a spirit wandering on the long road to the sky! But he was not one to strike and count coup while an enemy slept!

Now he was in the exact center of the camp; not one of the recumbent forms had stirred; and he saw before him what promised to be the goal of his expedition, for here was the long headdress of a chief, decked with eagle feathers, hanging from a suspended shield. Two lances were fixed in the ground side by side; each supported a shield; and from one hung the eagle feathers. On either side of those lances slept a warrior. Which, then, was the wearer of the headdress? Which was the leader of the bank? Thunder Moon leaned and stared fixedly at one and then at the other. Both were amazingly young, not far advanced into their twenties, so it seemed. But after all, fame on the warpath did not always accompany age. Youth sometimes would be served even on the blood trail across the plains.

He who seemed the older, and the more likely to be indeed the chief man of the party, lay, however, on the left of the spears. He who seemed the younger lay to their right, which seemed the more suitable position for the chief. And Thunder Moon, distracted, looked back to the moon, now sailing high through the black sea of night, putting out the stars as she traveled through the sky. But he received no sign to help him in his time of doubt. Close over the younger of the two he leaned and laid the point of his knife on the hollow of the sleeper's throat. Instantly the large eyes opened, and looked calmly up into the face of Thunder Moon.

"Pawnee," said he, speaking that tongue, "are you not the chief whom all these braves follow?"

The latter looked down at the glittering length of the knife blade.

"I am he!" he replied calmly.

The hand of Thunder Moon tightened on the haft of his weapon, but he could not strike. "Stand up—softly—and walk in front of me and out of the camp," he whispered. "I walk behind you, and in my hand I have six deaths!"

He touched the revolver at his thigh as he spoke; and without a word of protest or argument, the Pawnee rose, softly, as he had been bidden.

"If a man stirs, if a man groans," and Thunder Moon, "you are dead, Pawnee wolf!"

A loud burst of laughter rolled across to them from the nearest camp fire, where several young braves were seen routing out the sleepers. The heart of Thunder Moon stood still, and there was an expectant fear in the eyes of the youthful Pawnee as he glanced at the short gun that was now in the hand of his captor.

However, it was not the spreading of an alarm they had witnessed, but merely a fresh outbreak of rejoicing. And soon a dozen braves were capering around the fire and raising hideous war cries.

But the prisoner walked straight past the fire and the celebrants toward the edge of the camp, stepping with great care, for his way had to wind back and forth among the sleepers. They were nearly out of the camp when a sleeper wakened suddenly and raised himself upon one elbow. He looked full into the face of the prisoner—and raised his hands in a silent salutation.

Thunder Moon, making the same salute, followed—and felt the keen eyes of the Pawnee looking up at him.

They passed on, but, presently, Thunder Moon became aware that a man was following—a thing that he judged rather by guess than by sense-knowledge, for no sound was made by the feet of the trailer, and no shadow was cast by his coming. Yet Thunder Moon knew that there was danger behind him; and, turning a little as he wound between two prostrate forms, he risked a backward glance and saw that he who had recently saluted the young chief was now striding erect in his rear!

They passed the edge of the camp and descended into the little swale where Thunder Moon had slain the watcher who had risen out of the tall grass. Just before them and to the left were the horses, totally unguarded. For it seemed as though these Pawnees, by the greatness of their victory, felt that they had frightened all danger from the face of the prairies!

"Go toward the horses," said Thunder Moon to his captive, "and there pick out a pony and jump on its back, and take another horse by the leadrope."

For the ponies wandered here and there, the rawhide lariats trailing behind them. The captive gave no sign, but turned toward the horses and went on; tall, slender, lithe, stepping like a cat through the grass, so that his footfall made no sound even in its dry and crackling stems.

And from behind, equally catlike, curious, insistent, the other Pawnee stalked them without a spoken word. If Thunder Moon turned, the chief before him would whirl about and leap on his shoulders, wielding the short knife that was in his girdle. Or if Thunder Moon attempted first to dispose of the man ahead of him, the rifle that was in the hands of his trailer would instantly be fired into his back. He was in a quandary, and being cornered so deftly by ill chance, he determined to rely upon his spiritual protectors, the Sky People. Up to the ascending moon he raised his eyes, and as he looked down again, he saw his victim step aside and pick up the lead ropes of two ponies. They were admirable specimens of horseflesh; all the followers of the war chief in this raid had been mounted, as it appeared, upon specially chosen horses. The sides of these two had been heavily scored with whipstrokes that showed they had been ridden into the battle charge; but otherwise they seemed fresh, and lifted their heads and laid back their ears as the Pawnee approached them.

"Better bad spirit than no spirit at all!" thought Thunder Moon as he regarded those flattened ears.

"Brother," said a harsh and sudden voice close behind him, "what Pawnee wears long hair, like a woman or a dog of a Cheyenne?"

What to do then?

Thunder Moon, glancing before him, saw his captive sitting stiffly erect on the back of his pony, obviously ready to whirl and spring to the attack at the first opening. But better the attack of a man armed with a knife than the attack of one who carried a rifle!

"I shall tell you in one word!" said Thunder Moon quietly, and flicking the revolver from his thigh he only half turned and fired a snap shot under his left arm at the brave behind him. How many hundred times had he practiced that trick, and now his patience was rewarded! The Pawnee had his rifle at the ready with his finger on the trigger, and the weapon exploded as he fell with his forehead bored through by that well-aimed ball. The danger hissed close past the head of Thunder Moon, but he had no time to thank the Sky People for that escape from peril. He straightened to meet a shadow flying toward him through the air, for the young chief had swung around on the back of his pony and hurled himself like a projectile at his foe. And, as he leaped, he thrust before him with his knife.

Instinctively, Thunder Moon crouched and struck out and up with his left clenched fist. Over his head darted the knife of the Pawnee, a deadly ray of light, and at the same moment his whole arm went numb with the shock of the impact, and he felt his knuckles bite through flesh to the bone.

A limp, senseless form struck him, staggered him, and fell inert upon the ground at his feet, while the terribly loud echoes of the two explosions still rang through the swale with hollow, heavy voices.

The camp was already up. Stamp on the ground, and every wolf within a mile leaps to its feet; and the Pawnees were not less alert than sleeping wolves.

Up to their feet they started, weapons instantly in hand, and their shouts rose in a crash to the trembling moon. Then the foster son of Big Hard Face stooped to drive his knife into the heart of the fallen Pawnee chief, and he saw the young brave lying with his arms thrown above his head, his lips parted, and blood trickling down his cheek from the blow that had stunned him. There was no Cheyenne under the broad heavens who would have hesitated in a similar instance, but Thunder Moon could not strike the decisive blow.

Instead, he scooped up the limp body in one powerful arm, caught a frightened pony as it darted past, and threw his burden across its withers. He in turn mounted behind, and with the little beast groaning under the double weight, he forced it to gallop up the slope toward the trees. Like the promise of all blessing, the dark and obscuring shadows of the forest lay before him; and, as he reached its margin, he looked back and laughed through his teeth. Out from the camp came the first of the Pawnees to sight him as he vanished, but they were well to the rear; his own horse, fresh and strong, waited for him in the midst of the trees, and surely he had more than an even chance to make his escape—aye and carry his prisoner with him!

CHAPTER

7

He had a triple task before him when he got to his own pony. He had to wrench spear and shield from the ground; he had to tie his prisoner to his own saddle; and, leading his warhorse behind him, he had to ride the Pawnee pony on through the trees.

What he would do now, he had determined long before. Beyond the woods lay the broken district of a stretch of bad lands, and into that district, undoubtedly, the Pawnees would think that he had fled; whereas on the farther side of the little forest lay the river, and beyond the river there was nothing save the open, moonlit plains. Yet it was toward them that he headed, and as he rode, he heard the hunt crash past toward the hills, and he laughed again, savagely—a laughter that made no sound.

All was well in the heart of Thunder Moon when he reached the edge of the water, and saw that no one scouted on the farther bank. He rode boldly in, heedless in such a moment of a proper ford. At once the strong current foamed around the two swimming horses. They began to whirl around and around, their brave, pricked ears flattened, a sure sign of desperation in them; and Thunder Moon was about to strike out for himself toward the farther bank, when they struck a shallow sand bank, and in another moment were climbing the farther shore.

The captive, dazed, choking, coughing forth water from his lungs, had been brought back to his wits by that involuntary bath, but almost at once he whirled about as far as the rope permitted him to move to see in what manner he could annoy his captor.

He looked down along the great war spear of Thunder Moon, its narrow head glistening like eyes of vengeance. "If you cry out, friend," said Thunder Moon gravely, "I strike this spear through your heart and choke the noise you try to make."

The Pawnee stared at the spear point as though bewitched, and made no response.

But at length he murmured, "Tarawa, who rules in the top of the sky and the bottom of the earth, and who made everything and watches over everything—Tarawa has bewitched my brothers! He has veiled their eyes. Lo, there they ride! I see their shadows sweeping along the river and across the hills, and yet they will not look down and see me here!"

"Friend," answered Thunder Moon with satisfaction, "the eyes see only what the brain wishes them to know."

"It is true," groaned the young Pawnee, "and my brothers ride toward the hills to find me, never dreaming that you would dare to come by this open way! And you know it so well," he added, turning to Thunder Moon with wonder, "that you will not even gallop the horses!"

"If we rode fast, we would make a streak across the plain; the moonlight would glance on us, we would be discovered; but now we journey slowly, and the moon mist swallows us. We are no more than ghosts to them, already!"

He laughed again, but this time he allowed his voice to make a little sound; it rumbled deep in his throat, like an ominous music.

It seemed that the captive saw that all hope was lost for

him. He breathed deep, as though about to utter the war cry that would send the spear of his captor through his heart, but that also might doom his slayer to quick vengeance at the hands of the pursuing Pawnees. Yet, as the cry formed in his throat and at his lips, he looked again on the ready spear of Thunder Moon and checked the shout.

To the young, hope is a giant!

So they rode on, and finally, all sight and sound of the camp were lost behind them; the night grew older still; the wide silence of the plains received them, and in turn the cold gray of the dawn began to be sketched across the eastern horizon.

Now they reached a little rivulet, running not a hundred yards from its fountainhead before it sank into the thirsty prairie again, and here Thunder Moon looked to his captive, washed the blood from the wound his knuckles had made in the cheek of the Pawnee, and then freed him from the cruel strands of the rope.

"There is a long trail before us," said Thunder Moon. "Let us ride like friends. I have no pleasure in tormenting you. But all the while, I shall watch you. The little gun in my hand—you have seen that it does not strike in vain. So be warned, my friend!"

The Pawnee said nothing for some time after this. He kept his head high, yet it was plain that rage, shame, and despair were at work in him. He held his glance straight before him, and his jaw was set.

At length, Thunder Moon stopped to break his fast. He was no patient endurer of long famines, and now he knocked down two rabbits with expert shots of his revolver and paused to make a fire and cook the game.

The eyes of the Pawnee stared first at his captor, and then were slowly raised to follow the gradually ascending smoke that climbed the great arch of the sky.

Thunder Moon understood that surprised glance, but he said nothing. Only, when the rabbits were cooked, he offered one of them, neatly browned on a wooden spit, to the other.

The Pawnee stared again.

"My friend," said he in a pleasant and surprisingly gentle

voice, "in the towns of the Cheyennes, I know that the Pawnees are dogs and the sons of dogs; they are hated and they are feared; and one Pawnee scalp is more prized than five scalps of the Sioux or even more than a Comanche's! And yet—one does not stop to cook in the open prairie, when there may be danger on the trail—and offer the food to a dog. Is it true?"

"I am too hungry to think clearly," said Thunder Moon frankly. "You are hungry, also. Eat, my friend."

So they ate together, and from time to time Thunder Moon observed his captive. The longer he regarded him, the more certain he was that this was indeed the war chief; for even if the brave had not confessed his identity, there was about him such an air of dignity and grace as Thunder Moon never before had seen—not among the tall Cheyennes, not among the well-made Crows, or the graceful Blackfeet. The Pawnees tended to a broad and heavy build, as a rule; but this warrior was shaped with infinite skill, and his face, too, varied from the usual appearance of an Indian. It was more oval, the eyes were larger, and set in under a deep and thoughtful brow. And his features were molded with the same beauty and regularity with which his body was formed. He was such a man Thunder Moon felt fear never could come near this Pawnee, simply because fear was an ungraceful passion, unworthy of such a creature.

"Noble brother," said Thunder Moon at last, "I have heard the great chiefs of your nation named. Some of them I have met in battle, and I have seen them charge along the lines of the Cheyennes. But I have not seen you. You are as a stranger to me. Yet a tree does not grow from a slip to a great height in one day, and a man does not become great suddenly. Never have the Cheyennes been struck a blow as you struck them today. But tell me—where have you hidden yourself that you have not appeared before this upon the plains? And it is well for the Cheyennes that the fire is ended before it had a chance to consume them!"

The eyes of the captive glistened.

"It is well!" said he.

"Why do you call it well?" asked Thunder Moon naively.

"Is it well that you should be here with me, journeying where I am to take you?"

"Where I go," said the Pawnee, "is a small thing. Where I travel, the Pawnees will hardly care. Only one man among them will yearn for me greatly."

Thunder Moon stared.

"I have spoken!" ended the other.

"You have spoken strangely," declared Thunder Moon. "Are the Pawnees worse than wolves in winter who eat their dead? Do they forget their great men as soon as they have fallen?"

"No," said the youth, "but I have done no great deeds. If I have counted seven coups—why, that is not many. If I have slain four men in battle, that also is not much. But it is well that all the four were Cheyennes. Their spirits are lost between earth and heaven. But their scalps will hang in my lodge and dry there in the smoke; and their medicine bags and their souls in them shall be sacrificed to Tarawa."

Thunder Moon fondled the shaft of his long knife with a loving touch, and at the same time regarded the other with a melancholy eye.

"Look, my friend," said he. "You walk now on a dangerous trail. But still I listen. Your words I cannot altogether understand. That man who led the Pawnees in the battle of yesterday is no unskillful warrior. What if no more than four men have fallen before his hand? The brain is mightier than the arm, both in the council and in the battle. And though he never strikes a single blow himself, he would have caused the death of hundreds of the enemies of his people if he had lived. If he had lived!" added Thunder Moon, and dwelt upon the Pawnee with an infinite satisfaction.

However, the latter seemed not a whit dismayed. He even laughed a little, softly and deeply in his throat, as a man will do when he exults greatly.

"And he lives, and the hundreds of whom you speak shall fall. He will wash the prairies with blood, even for my sake!"

"For your sake?" echoed Thunder Moon.

"For my sake, Cheyenne! Because I told you that I was the

leader, when you leaned above me, your knife at my throat, does it follow that I am the chief in fact?''

Thunder Moon was silent, watching with burning eyes. Truth and ecstasy of great accomplishment were stamped upon the face and trembling in the voice of the Pawnee.

''For if I had denied, your knife would have turned from me and entered the heart of the son of my father!''

''The son of your father!''

''Falling Stone! Falling Stone is my brother and our leader! It was he who washed his hands in the blood of the best of the Cheyennes yesterday. And he still lives, and he shall not die until he has swept the Cheyennes howling from the plains and driven them into the Father of Waters. I have spoken! Open the sky, and Tarawa strike me if I have not told the truth—if I have not made a prophecy!''

CHAPTER

8

Very great had been the hopes Thunder Moon had founded upon that midnight exploit of his. Now he found his hopes dashed quite to the ground; and his heart swelled in him with disappointment, first, and then with a deadly rage against his companion.

"Traitor—dog of a Pawnee!" gasped he, and he lurched a little forward, and caught the shoulder of the youth in that terrible clasp that the strongest men of the Cheyennes knew so well and feared so much—that grip that, as men say, in the midst of battle, when all other weapons were broken or lost, had served him to tear the life out of a foeman as you or I might pluck out the core from an orange!

But the Pawnee endured that grip, though the iron finger-tips were biting through his flesh and grinding the nerves against the bone. He endured it, and although the sweat started upon his forehead, he smiled calmly, proudly, even disdainfully upon Thunder Moon.

"Strike when you will, friend," said the Pawnee. "I have

told you the truth. That is a snake that only bites the heel of a villain. And I have seen you stung!''

It was, on the whole, as well rounded an insult as could have been flung in the face of a Cheyenne, and Thunder Moon gasped deeply with fury. Twice the long blade of his hunting knife gleamed naked of the sheath, and twice he thrust it back within the leather. At last, he sat back, frowning.

"You see the torture before you," he said, "and you see the Cheyenne women—whose fathers and brothers and sons have fallen by your hand and by the weapons of your men—you see them gathered around you, tearing your flesh, burning you, filling your ears with taunts, dangling before your face your own scalp. And, therefore, the greater the chief the greater the torment. So you would belie yourself, discard your name, and take another. But that is the game of a child, and I smile at you, and understand the trick!''

"You lie," replied the Pawnee, with a sneer. "As I hang on the stake I shall laugh at the Cheyenne she-devils as they tear me; and I shall laugh when my own scalp is dangled in my face; and, until death chokes me, I shall shout out the names of the Cheyenne warriors who have fallen under my hand. I shall laugh and sing my battle song and my death song, and make my boast true in the ears of men and in the ears of Tarawa who hears all things!''

He looked up, and smiled at the sun-flooded sky.

Thunder Moon listened, aghast, for now he felt that he had heard the truth, indeed. And so this great exploit, this greatest of his deeds, was a useless thing!

He sighed bitterly.

"I have asked too much," said he. "The Sky People heard only a part of my prayer!"

"Brother," said the Pawnee with the same disdainful smile, "did you think that the Sky People to whom you prayed could have filled your hands with such glory as the death of Falling Stone? No, he is a warrior who is not fated to die in such manner. When he falls, thousands shall fall around him! Wait but a little and you shall have a sign from him. For he comes across the prairies swifter than a great fire, scourged along by the wind. The horses die under him as he rides. And he sings a terrible song in his heart: 'My brother, Rising Cloud, is lost to me! A thousand men shall die for his sake!' ''

As he spoke, he swept his hand toward the horizon, and Thunder Moon, so had the words worked upon him, started a little, and bit his lip when he saw that he had shown his emotion. But, for that matter, he never had been able to control his expression with the true immobility of feature that distinguishes an Indian of pure blood.

"Words are not bullets," said Thunder Moon dryly, "and speeches are not armed warriors charging together. It may be that some day I shall meet this Falling Stone, this brother, and there shall be mourning in the lodge of your father and your mother again. There are some who reap glory and gather it like corn, and preserve it like pemmican; but others take what has been reaped and what has been preserved and it is they who eat it. But you, Rising Cloud, you are young, and yet you are very brave."

The Pawnee was so amazed by this compliment that he was utterly speechless for a long moment.

"You are brave," said Thunder Moon, speaking his thoughts aloud, rather than addressing his prisoner directly, "and you are wise, as well. You were wise in what you said to me; also, what courage is greater than for a man to die for another—even for his brother?"

He paused.

"And a thought comes to me," said Thunder Moon continuing. "It may be that you will not die under the hands of the squaws and the children, while the Cheyenne braves look on. I have promised a sacrifice to the Sky People who brought me safely into the camp of Falling Stone and took me out again. It might be, Rising Cloud, that you would be a sacrifice acceptable to them. I would not sacrifice a scalped and dishonored man. How could a wandering ghost be acceptable to them? One who had lost his medicine bag and his soul? One who could not ride in the plains above us and follow the buffalo over the shadows in the sky? So I have this thought, Rising Cloud, of dressing you in all the regalia of a great Pawnee chief and then striking you dead as an offering to the

Sky People. After that, I would bury you honorably, and kill a fine horse beneath the frame on which your body lay, and put weapons beside you, even good rifles and knives, and all that a spirit could need in the hereafter!''

When he had finished this singular speech, Rising Cloud maintained an erect head for a moment only, and then his glance dropped to the ground. In this manner they remained for some time, the foster son of the Cheyenne turning his thought in his mind and finding it good, and the Pawnee apparently overcome by this generous offer. A death by indescribable torment had lain before him; and to avoid it he had badgered this pale-skinned enemy in the hope of provoking a sudden thrust of the knife. Now, however, he was promised an end almost as honorable as death in the midst of battle, charging at the side of one's best friends for the honor of the tribe.

"How many," asked the Pawnee suddenly, "died in the camp of my brother last night? From how many did you take the medicine bags?"

"Three," said Thunder Moon, and went on with his secret thoughts calmly.

"Three men died under your hand, and a fourth was carried away a prisoner like a child or a helpless woman!" said the Pawnee, writhing with shame. "But," he added, raising his head again, "it is plain that the Sky People gave you power. Tarawa willed it. He would not have the Pawnees too proud. He wished to tame the high spirit of Falling Stone after the great victory! And so he chose the hand of Thunder Moon, who is the heart and the head and the hand of the Cheyennes!"

At this, the big man looked up sharply.

"How do you know my name, brother?" he asked.

"The wolf kills in one way," said the Pawnee, "and the mountain lion does not have two ways of killing the deer. Have I not heard the story of how a Cheyenne rode far south to the camp of the Comanches and killed in that camp and brought away the greatest medicine of the tribe?"

"So!" breathed Thunder Moon. "And that is known even to the Pawnees!"

"Besides," said the young brave, and he smiled a little, "I have not heard that there are two Cheyennes with pale faces and with hands of iron. We know you, brother. When I looked up from my sleep and saw the glittering of your knife, had it been any other man, I should have struck one blow for my life and to alarm the camp. But I saw that it was Thunder Moon, and I gave up hope."

The delicious sweetness of praise ran softly and kindly into the soul of Thunder Moon, but he controlled himself and said merely, "It is time that we take the trail once more!"

So they mounted and resumed their way across the plains, refreshed. They continued through the day, goading the sides of their weary horses. The hot sun dipped into the western haze; it set, and the sky was covered with delicate color. Immediately afterward, they could see dim lights twinkling before them and, coming closer, they saw the Cheyenne village spread out before them.

It was always a noisy time of the day, for it was the moment when the boys, bringing in the horses they had herded and guarded during the day, swept with whoops and yells into the camp. It was the time, too, when the braves went forth often and shouted their invitations to a feast. And there was the neighing of horses, and their frightened snorting as they were tethered for the night near by. Now, however, all these sounds were lacking; but first, from the distance, it seemed that one long, shrill voice was wailing out of the edge of the sky, and as the two drew closer they heard this sound dissolved into many portions, and each was the lament of a woman, sharp and thin, and reaching over the prairie as far as the cry of a hunting wolf.

"You hear?" said Thunder Moon grimly. "It is a token that Falling Stone is not forgotten in the city of the Suhtai. And when you enter that place with me, you ride into great danger, my brother. Yet keep a strong heart. I shall not forsake you. Ride before me. Go slowly, and yet never stop, even if a crowd gathers close before your horse. Ride straight into the center of the village, and when you see a bear lodge, with a great red bear painted along the side of it with wonderful art, you will know that that is the home of my father, December. Go to that lodge and dismount. I shall be close behind you, protecting you."

"It is well," said the Pawnee. "And yet," he added wistfully, "if you will sacrifice me to the Sky People who are your friends, Tarawa who hears all things and sees all things is as near to us now as he will be in the center of the Cheyenne camp. Strike now, Thunder Moon, and accomplish your vow, for if you take me into the village, the women who have lost husbands and sons in the battle will tear me out of your hands. I have seen such things happen! I know them very well!"

"Brother," said Thunder Moon calmly, "I am not a young man. Among the Cheyennes my name is known. I do not take you in among my people in order to shame you or put you in danger of the devilish hands of the women. But there is another purpose you serve in coming with me into the camp of the Cheyennes. I have to prove that one man there is a liar. After that is done, have no fear. You shall die simply and quickly!"

"It is well," repeated the Pawnee.

CHAPTER

9

At the edge of the village, the wailing of the women had increased in volume and become wildly poignant cries, each with its separate, hoarse note of woe. There Thunder Moon paused, and taking his robe from his own shoulders he threw it around those of his companion.

"Because," said he, "it is not good that a great man and a chief should be naked before the eyes of strangers!"

Rising Cloud gave his captor a single glance brimming and brilliant with gratitude, and then they entered the camp. They had made no other preparation, except that Thunder Moon had tied to his lance, near its point, the three medicine bags he had taken from his victims in the Pawnee camp. These dangled, strange small shapes—one was the tiny skin of a field mouse; one was the pelt of a small muskrat; one was the soft hide of a chipmunk. In them were who could tell what odd trinkets, the collection of which had been commanded by the same dreams that made the warriors who had owned these bags in the first place go out to collect them; and there was about them, in spite of their small size and their strange appearance, a mysterious importance, at least, in the eyes of all who knew their significance. For they were, almost literally, the souls of men—the souls of dead men, still lingering upon the earth in this form. And, no matter how bravely the hero might have died, no matter with what perfect ceremonies he were buried, still, because he had lost his medicine bag, all peace was stolen from his spirit forever.

There was such excitement through the village, however, that no attention was paid to the two horsemen, for they were only now and again illumined by the light that came flooding out from some bright fire within a lodge whose flap hung open. And so they had covered almost half the distance to the center of the town, when the harsh, crackling voice of an old man sang out, "The medicine of Spotted Bull lied when it said that Thunder Moon would not return to the Suhtai. It lied, for here is Thunder Moon, and he brings a companion with him!"

Straight before them, at that moment, was a woman seated in the middle of the way, cross-legged, covered with dirt. Her long hair she had shorn away with slashes of a knife, and some of those cuts had gashed her scalp and let the blood flow. Furthermore, she had slashed her legs and arms and breast with the same knife, which she still brandished in her hand and which she sometimes struck into the earth and sometimes waved over her head, all the while keeping up a terrible keening. Often it was a wordless lament. But again, it took shape in words: "Sky People, under earth spirits, spirits that live in the water, how did Big River hurt you? When was he not your friend? But you deserted him. You went from him. Then you held his arms so that he could not strike the Pawnee wolf who came and tore at his breast. Yet his heart was great. He would not die even from such a terrible wound. He kept fighting. But you wanted to have him dead. You held his arms, and two more Pawnee devils leaped on him and bore him down. He lies far off on the plains. The river has rolled him ashore like a dead pebble. His body is filled with water. And I am here! Pity me! Take my life from me quickly! Carry me away to Big River! There let my soul dwindle and fade from the earth with his soul, until both become so thin that even the eye of Tarawa cannot see us! Let me die! I do not wish to live! My lodge is empty and the pipe that hangs from the lodge pole never will be smoked again!''

In this manner she lamented, and all these exclamations were interspersed with wild, long-drawn, animal-like cries and howls, and then heartbroken sobbings. However, now she heard the name of Thunder Moon, and it startled her to her feet. Up she bounded, knife in hand, and throwing herself down before the warrior she literally embraced the knees of his tired pony. Which, except for its weariness, would have trampled her into the ground.

"I cried out!" she screamed up to the brave. "I cried out, and the spirits heard me, and they sent me Thunder Moon. Oh, Thunder Moon, Spotted Bull lied when he said that you would not return to us. He lied, too, when he sent our braves out and would not let you lead them. May he die—may he rot like mildewed meat! For if you had led our warriors, they never would have been beaten. No, they would be riding back now with scalps at their bridles. They would be dancing around the fires, counting their coups! Oh, may Spotted Bull shrivel away like grass in the first heats! May he—''

Here two other women rushed to her and tried to cover her mouth with their hands, cautioning her, begging her not to bring her soul into mortal peril by challenging the wrath of the medicine man.

"He dares not touch me, the liar and cheat, the mangy dog, Spotted Bull! For Thunder Moon is here. To my husband he was a brother. When Thunder Moon and Big River rode out together, they made the Pawnees tremble. But Spotted Bull separated them, and therefore let him die and be shamed before all men and let—'' She broke off and added, "Thunder Moon, Thunder Moon, my husband's friend, be a friend to me!''

"I am your friend," said the warrior gently.

"Then go to the river, find his body; take me to find his body and bury it. The same water that took his dead body, let it take my dead one, and so my soul shall float down the stream and come to his soul!''

Before an answer could be given, through the crowd that

had begun to gather a loud voice sounded: "Who is the fool who curses Spotted Bull and wishes for his death? Who is she?" And Spotted Bull himself came striding through the crowd, who gave way before him.

He came directly to the squaw of Big River and she cringed away from him, taking shelter between her two companions; but even these seemed quite anxious to get away from her, and tried vainly to disengage the hands with which she clutched them so firmly.

"The going of Big River may have been only a token and a sign," said Spotted Bull, extending his clenched hand over the squaw. "But bring two good horses and tie them to the post in front of my lodge. It may be that I may be able to intercede with the Sky People and turn their anger away from you because you have cursed me. But unless—"

Hundreds had gathered and still were gathering. The space between the tepees was jammed tight with men and women and children, so that the Pawnee, trying to get ahead through the mob, found himself lodged there, and helpless, unable to move.

And here the stern voice of Thunder Moon broke in. "Spotted Bull, spotted calf, spotted coyote, take your hand from the woman. I have come back to let the Cheyennes know that you are a liar and a fool! Do not look at the squaw of Big River whom you sent out to death with the other warriors. Look to me. You gave them weak medicine. You put a curse on me; but your medicine was nothing. The Sky People laughed at you. And here are medicine bags of the Pawnees to prove that I have been among them!"

Spotted Bull, who had stormed up to the squaw in such a passion that he had been blind to all other faces and forms, now looked up to the towering silhouette of the man on horseback. And at that instant the flap of an adjoining tepee was thrown open, and a flickering, wild firelight streamed out upon the face of Thunder Moon. So Spotted Bull went backward a step, staggering like one who has received a heavy blow. And a sort of groan of interest and of fear came from the lips of the crowd. For it was a terrible thing to which they had listened—never before in the annals of the Suhtai had a chief medicine man been denounced in the face of the entire tribe in this fashion.

He recovered himself almost at once, however, for he was one who made his living as an actor, and by the constant use of words. And he called out, pointing to the medicine bags that dangled from the head of the war spear of the brave, "After the bear has fought and feasted, the buzzards steal down from the sky and eat also! You have sneaked up into the battlefield. You have found dead Pawnees and stolen their medicine bags before their friends could bury them! Now you come here and talk loudly, but men know that every liar has a huge voice!"

There was another gasp from the crowd. They seemed to think that the spear of Thunder Moon would be buried in the breast of the medicine man the next instant. And so, doubtless, it would have been, had Spotted Bull carried a gun or even a knife. But as it was, he stood defenseless before the warrior, showing such courage as few men in the tribe would have exhibited at such a moment.

"I have not come back here to murder you, Spotted Bull," said Thunder Moon. "But I have come back to kill your reputation. I shall make you laughed at even by the children. Your own squaws will scorn you and spit on you. Do you say that I have not been in the camp of the Pawnees?"

"I say it, and I know it," went on the medicine man, boldly brazening out the situation, for he saw that either he or Thunder Moon must go down on this occasion.

"By your medicine you know it?" asked Thunder Moon in a dry voice.

There was not so much as the whispering sound of a drawn breath through all the crowd. Never before had they come to a moment of such terrible interest. For no warrior in their tribe was so great as Thunder Moon; and no medicine man had such a reputation as Spotted Bull. How often his medicine had brought rain! How often his medicine had sent them out to successful battle or to good hunting! It was now the meeting, as it were, of flesh and spirit. And great things were expected.

"Yes," said the medicine man. "I talked to the spirits. A

spirit came like an owl and sat on my shoulder and told me that you had crept out onto the battlefield and tried to steal a great name by taking these three medicine bags.''

"Hear me, Spotted Bull," said Thunder Moon. "Do you know the name of the chief of the Pawnees who led the army?''

"It is Falling Stone. The spirits have told me. They told me after the braves started on the trail. I tried to call them back to tell them that the Sky People had given luck to the Pawnees. All that happened was revealed to me—and that included your wretched treachery!''

"That is not true!" shrilled the sudden voice of the squaw of Big River. "When has Thunder Moon lied in all his life?''

CHAPTER

10

"Woman," cried the medicine man to the squaw, "because you made your husband sin, he died. Now you draw down on your head the—"

"Harken to me, Spotted Bull," broke in Thunder Moon. "You have told me the name of the chief of the Pawnees. Have the spirits told you the name of his brother, also?"

"What is that? I ask only for the chief leader," replied the medicine man.

"But I shall tell you the name of Falling Stone's brother. Do you wish to know?"

Spotted Bull stretched out his long arm and shook his finger toward Thunder Moon.

"Hear this man, oh my brothers!" he cried. "With the heart and the soul of a liar, he is striving to turn your minds to other things—small things—while he juggles his words and makes small matters into great ones, so that you may forget him and his lies!"

"I shall tell you," said Thunder Moon, "that the brother of the war chief of the Pawnees also is a great warrior. The scalps of four Cheyennes dry now in his tent. And his name is Rising Cloud.''

''More lies!'' said the medicine man. ''I smell them afar like a carrion that has lain a fortnight on the ground and in the sun. More lies!''

''They are truths,'' answered Thunder Moon. ''Now I shall shut your mouth forever, Spotted Bull, and make you less than a starved dog in this camp, less than a toothless old dog that no longer can crack a bone! Do you hear me? Do you hear me, all my friends of the Suhtai? There sits Rising Cloud on that horse, wrapped in his robe. The medicine of Spotted Bull was fool's medicine. He sent out your young men to their death. But, in spite of him, I went behind the war party. I came up and saw them fleeing from the river. Then I crossed the river and went into the woods that stood on the hills near the camp of the Pawnees. I was so close that their howling for the victory filled my ears. Then I went down into their camp to get their best man, their leader. By chance I missed him. The moon spirit and the Sky People helped me and brought me to the right place, but there like a blind man I failed to see the war chief. But I brought away a brave warrior, his brother, as a proof that Spotted Bull is a fool and a coward, and that his medicine is weaker than water!''

As though to verify what had been said, at this moment Rising Cloud allowed the robe to fall away from his head, and the familiar headdress of a Pawnee was instantly recognized. A howl of wonder and delight went up from all in the crowd, and that howl, like a roaring voice of fate, silenced Spotted Bull.

He shrank back, scowling and muttering. And as others pressed forward, he allowed himself to drift toward the rear, and presently disappeared, to skulk softly away toward his own lodge and there sit with his robe gathered about his head, speaking not at all, while his frightened wives moved like shadows here and talked with one another by the sign language.

However, now that the mass of listening, excited Cheyennes stirred before them, Thunder Moon pressed ahead, and carried the young prisoner with him. They managed to make their way only with great difficulty. The warriors were sullen

and silent, for the most part, as they saw the prisoner go past
them. The younger men and boys screamed with pleasure and
almost forgot the greatness of the defeat in this sight. But the
danger was from the women who had lost kin in the battle.

Knives flashed and clubs were swung up on either hand,
and many a deadly blow would have been directed at the
Pawnee if it had not been for the thundering voice of his
captor, following rapidly in the rear and calling to the Suhtai
women to beware.

"If there is harm done to the Pawnee," Thunder Moon
shouted, "I shall take vengeance for it, blood for blood, and
head for head! Beware and keep back! The Sky People have
sent him to us. Let us treat him as a gift from heaven!"

Thus calling out, he managed to keep Rising Cloud from
harm; and so they pressed on through a growing pandemoni-
um until they came to the central portion of the village, and
there reached the lodge of Big Hard Face, with the walking
bear painted in brilliant red upon it.

The old man was standing at the flap of the tepee, his arms
folded inside his robe. It fitted neither his position nor his age
to rush away and mingle with the curious to learn the news,
but his eyes were flashing. For he had heard the name of
Thunder Moon shouted, and he could not tell in what
connection—whether it meant news of life or news of death—
until he saw the familiar great shoulders of the rider breaking
through the mass, and the Pawnee herded before him.

Then he started violently, and raised a hand in salutation.
He permitted himself no word of triumph or of exultation,
merely gathering his arms again inside his robe, while his
foster son dismounted. And indeed, whether emotion had
mastered him or he wished to appear indifferent, he turned
and disappeared into the tepee, where his son and the prisoner
immediately followed him.

Only White Crow remained outside the lodge. All the life
of Thunder Moon, since first he had been brought, a crying
infant, to the lodge of Big Hard Face, White Crow had been
divided between interest and pride on the one hand, and
aversion on the other. This was no child of her childless body;
neither was it a child of her nephew, Big Hard Face. There-

fore, she detested Thunder Moon and all the ways in which his white blood appeared. On that score she never ceased badgering the chief about his foster son. But, on the other hand, her breast swelled with joy and pride because of the exploits of this young warrior who rode out from her tepee. So she remained outside the lodge, boasting in a loud, shrill voice, taunting her neighbors by name.

"Who has gone out from your lodge, Wind Woman, and brought back glory and prisoners? Red Leaf, who is it that has gone out from your lodge and done such things? But I send out Thunder Moon. A great, bright moon that blinds the eyes of the Pawnees. And like a thunderstorm he strikes them down. They shrink before him. He leans from his horse and picks up their chief men and brings them back with him like antelope meat!"

In this manner she boasted.

Presently the head men of the Suhtai began to arrive at the tepee, and one by one they passed inside the home of their old chief. Excitement waxed constantly in the gathering crowd. There the women who mourned for dead kinsmen had drawn to the front, covered with blood from the gashes they had inflicted upon one another; their clothes in rent rags, their bodies covered with dust and with ashes; but now they had forgotten their laments and with one voice they demanded that the prisoner be led forth and delivered over into their hands. He was their due. They had earned the right to send his soul on the long journey with all the cunning torments their hands could devise! So they shouted, and the shrill voice of White Crow boasted, as she walked back and forth in front of the tepee.

Inside, there was another scene. Guarded by two famous warriors, the prisoner sat cross-legged at one side; his face utterly immobile, his fine eyes apparently unconscious of the keen, cruel glances that were fixed upon him, and his ears apparently unaware of the debate that raged concerning him.

First of all, as was his duty, but with perfect simplicity and without boasting, Thunder Moon told a straightforward tale of how he had approached the Pawnee camp, watched it, listened to the songs and shoutings of his enemy, and then made his prayer to the Sky People and his guardian spirit in the moon; how he had struck down the forager for wood; how he had gone into the camp and killed a watcher on the way; how he had gained the central place and found the insignia of the chief; how he had taken the wrong man, as it appeared; how he had led him out and been followed by a suspicious Pawnee; how he had killed this man, also, and how he had finally escaped almost by miracle from the swarming Pawnee hunters who rode to find him. Here, then, was the prisoner. For his part, he had a mind to lead out the chief at the next moonrise and sacrifice him in return for the aid the Sky People had given to him. But this was a matter in which the wise men of the tribe should first be consulted.

The old chief had the right of first speech, but he shook his head and bade others offer their opinions.

Snake-that-talks—a young man but a famous fighter, and long ago a companion of Thunder Moon on a famous war trail that carried him deep into the country of the Comanches— was the first to speak and he said, "A scalp is a scalp and a coup is good to count. Besides, the women deserve to have sport with this man. And, more than this, it will gladden the spirits of many unhappy Cheyennes who now are wandering spirits, drifting here and there about that river where they died. It will gladden them to see a Pawnee ghost come so quickly to join them! Let Rising Cloud be given to the women—only let Thunder Moon count coup upon him three times and take his scalp when the women have ended their pleasure with him!"

Thunder Moon, listening, leaned forward and looked intently into the face of the captive, but the latter gave no sign that he had heard this terrible advice. Most of the others agreed to this scheme, except Gray Eagle, who declared that some good might be done the tribe by trading the prisoner back to the Pawnees, because the war chief, Falling Stone, doubtless would pay an enormous price to redeem his brother.

"Brother," said old December, at this point, "all the horses and all the buffalo on the plains could not pay us for the men we have lost. Our young men, too, will grow afraid of the Pawnees after this battle unless they see a fresh scalp before long. Give us Rising Cloud, my son. Let us do what we will with him! Let the women have him, saving only his scalp for you!''

Twice Thunder Moon attempted to speak, and twice his voice failed him. He could not withdraw his eyes from the handsome, immobile face of his captive. But at length he said, ''This is not a little thing. I have promised a great sacrifice to the Sky People. Let me have until tomorrow to think about this thing. As for the women,'' he added with a sudden flash of disgust, ''they yell like coyotes. Let them wait. I shall tell them my thoughts later!''

CHAPTER

11

It is necessary to go back to the raid of the Pawnees to describe a most important detail that now had bearing upon the course of events.

When Falling Stone and his band swept down upon the Cheyenne village, they carried away with them a great portion of the horses of the Suhtai; and they even made some lucky inroads upon the band of Thunder Moon's Comanche ponies. But the tribe underwent a loss more mortal than that of men or ponies.

Long ago, when Big Hard Face came back from his foray carrying his white foster son in his arms, he was riding upon a tall dark chestnut stallion, taken from a breeder of thoroughbreds, with blood as pure and an ancestry more ancient than the blood of kings. That great horse became the father of a line of such stock as plain Indians never had backed before. Hardy as the Indian ponies, but with galloping powers far beyond the stretch of the pony legs, the chestnuts had served to mount Thunder Moon's band on that famous occasion when he foraged deep in the territory of the Comanches and had scoured away from all pursuit. Upon one of those chestnuts, therefore, he would have been mounted at the time of the Pawnee foray had it not been that these chosen animals had been put out to graze, under careful guard, at a distance from the camp. There they were safe enough, it seemed. Trained and schooled more carefully than the Indian children themselves, these horses came at a whistle and obeyed the voice almost as though they understood human speech. Therefore, they could not be stampeded. And on two occasions when skillful thieves had managed to get on the back of one of December's chestnuts, the faithful animals had come back to the call of their master and brought their would-be captors with them. So it was considered safe enough to range the horses at a distance from the camp, under a guard of three or four men, keeping them always where the choicest grass was to be found. But on the very night when Thunder Moon returned with his prisoner, disastrous tidings were brought in that the impossible had been accomplished, and that five of the chestnuts had been taken in the dusk of that same day—taken by a sort of magic, as it appeared, and spirited away from the hollow in which they were grazing. The guards made only a feeble effort to follow the trail when they noticed the loss. Darkness closed on the prairie. So they came back to report the loss.

Five out of twelve magnificent horses were gone, and the guards dared not go directly to Big Hard Face, but came and touched the feet of Thunder Moon as he lay asleep. To him they told their story and he in turn took heart and reported the tragedy to his father. There had been no sign of any danger on the plains, the herdsmen reported. Only, in the late afternoon, a great buffalo wolf had been observed sitting on the top of a distant hummock.

"It was no wolf, but a Pawnee!" declared Big Hard Face instantly.

And straightway, he and Thunder Moon, and half a dozen of the best trailers in the tribe, made ready to mount the remaining chestnuts and start the pursuit. But they made their preparations with heavy hearts. They were far behind. The dark had passed and the dawn had come since the thief made off with his prizes. Scarcely ten days of hard riding could make up for the difference, even with the best of luck.

But while the preparations for departure were under way, an event happened that filled the mind of Thunder Moon with something other than troubles about horseflesh.

Already, in the rosy light of the morning, the squaws were beginning their keening at a distance from the camp, and the melancholy sounds came from afar off in the saddest of music, when Thunder Moon, standing in front of his foster father's lodge, heard a tumult down the main passage through the tepees and presently he saw the Omissis, Walking Horse, riding toward him.

A little crowd was running out to look at the chief, then hastily forming in behind him. But it seemed to Thunder Moon that their attention was not so much fixed upon the Omissis as upon something behind him. A little later, he could see that a woman followed the chief; and now, as the pair drew closer, he could see that it was such a woman as never before had entered the Suhtai camp.

For she had long, red hair, and even from a distance it flashed like two copper swords, curving down from her brows and over her shoulders in massive braids. Her skin was not so swarthy as that of an Indian belle, but was a rich, dark olive; and, though she was not tall, she carried herself in such a manner that she filled the eye entirely. Thunder Moon never had seen a creature quite like her in all the days of his life.

In the meantime, the Omissis came to the lodge entrance and there halted. He dismounted and saluted Thunder Moon, and Big Hard Face, who had just come out.

"Brothers," he said, smiling upon them, "I have come back, and I have brought the payment for the fifty horses, as we planned and bargained together!"

So saying, he pointed to a whole string of pack ponies now approaching, driven forward by several of Walking Horse's tribesmen. The arrival of such a cargo put off even the thoughts of redeeming the five lost chestnuts.

Now the pack ponies came up, and one by one they were unloaded of such treasure as rarely had come under the eye of an Indian in one bulk. There were nearly a hundred rifles;

there were quantities of powder and lead; there were five six-shooters of the new Colt pattern—miracle guns they seemed to the Cheyennes, even though they had watched them at work in the hands of Thunder Moon, for his shooting with them was considered rather as "medicine" than as the use of a weapon. Besides, there were plaited robes and beaded suits, and excellent knives, and indeed, all that could gladden the heart of a Suhtai.

In heaps this treasure was carried into the lodge of December, and White Crow received it, gloating over its masses.

"We are to take all of this," said Big Hard Face, "and in return, you wish no horses?"

"I have made the bargain," said Walking Horse, "and I have received your word under witness of Tarawa. You will accept in turn what I am to give you and keep it in your tepee—you and Thunder Moon—you will guard it carefully?"

"That is all agreed," said Big Hard Face impatiently. "And now, brother, what is the thing?"

Walking Horse turned sharply around and made an imperious gesture.

The girl at once dismounted and taking her hand Walking Horse placed it in the hand of Thunder Moon.

"Other men," said he, "accept great gifts for a daughter, and especially for a beautiful girl. But, instead, I offer the price of fifty horses to the man who will accept her. Her name is Red Wind. Take her as you have sworn to do. Put her in your lodge. Guard her well and keep her. Make her your squaw if you will. But watch her always."

Thunder Moon was stunned. He looked down to the soft, slender hand that lay in his; he looked up to the face of the girl, and saw that her eyes were not black, but the deepest, darkest shade of blue, like the color of water at dusk—almost like the color of the midnight sky.

They passed into the tepee. Big Hard Face, his doubts ended, began to laugh a little, and his old eyes shone as he looked to Walking Horse.

"Brother," said he, "you have given us two gifts, and the first was worth fifty fine horses; but the second looks to me still more valuable."

Walking Horse, in place of replying, smiled most sourly. Then he turned on the girl.

"I have brought you into a new life," he said to her in a stern voice. "Among the Omissis, you have made much trouble. Twenty men have had their knives ready for my throat because of you. There has been no peace among us for five years. Now I take you to another tribe. Guard your voice. Take heed when you sing. Keep your head covered. Learn cookery and the dressing of skins. And it may be that you will become a blessing to Thunder Moon. But make such trouble in his lodge as you have made in mine, and be sure that he will take you with one hand and crush out your life as a boy catches a small bird and crushes it to death. I have spoken!"

And, with this bitter farewell, he turned upon his heel and left the tepee. Big Hard Face overtook him just outside.

"Walking Horse," said he, "we are friends. And when two friends are together, they point out to one another the dangers that threaten him. Now, you see a danger. You see that there is a storm ahead, but Thunder Moon and I cannot see it. Tell us, then, from what direction it may blow."

"I shall tell you," said Walking Horse, half sternly and half in sorrow. "From this moment, there is danger all around you. It lies down by your side at night, it walks beside you in the day. It steals up behind you in the dusk. It slides in the shadow of your galloping horse, and it hangs in the sky above you. Danger blows toward you from every corner of the sky!"

Big Hard Face became sober indeed.

"Brother," he entreated, "we look and we see only a beautiful girl. The color of her hair is strange. But it is not unpleasant. Otherwise, she seems what a woman should be. Tell us, therefore, in what way she may harm us?"

"You are not a young man," said the Omissis, unrelenting. "I am not a boy, and yet you could be my father. You are the chief who leads a great tribe, and the councils of Big Hard Face have made the Suhtai rich and great on the plains. You have a great warrior in your lodge. There is no other like him among all the Cheyennes. Between you, you may discover the danger for yourselves. It may be that no danger at all will be seen. The Sky People listen to the voice of Thunder Moon. They may teach him what to do and how to make a wild bird sing songs. But now I have been long from my people and they need me. We have been in great trouble. I have lived for five years with the knife at my throat. Now I shall go back to my lodge and lie down to a long sleep. Farewell! Be wise, and let White Crow keep her eyes open every day and every night!''

With this, he turned away and mounted his horse and was gone, followed instantly by the Omissis who had driven in the pack train.

CHAPTER

12

The pursuit of the five lost horses was forgotten. Thunder Moon went back into the lodge and found the maiden standing with her hands folded together as close to the wall of the tepee as she could get. The prisoner, Rising Cloud, turned the eyes that had been watching her toward his captor, and it seemed to the latter that there was a touch of keen envy in the expression of the Pawnee.

"You have ridden on a long trail," said Thunder Moon to the girl. "Sit down. White Crow, put meat before her."

"This is fitting!" said the old hag, her withered face growing black with anger. "I must wait on a slave who has been given away by her own father because of the evil that is in her! I must wait on her! I shall not lift my hand to help her!"

"It is true that I must serve myself," said the girl meekly, and would have risen, but Thunder Moon with a gesture made her sit down again.

"What evil is there in her?" he asked his foster aunt.

The hag went to the girl with long strides, and laid hold on a heavy coil of the copper-red hair.

"There is danger in this, worse than fire!" she said.

"Fire?" murmured Thunder Moon, astonished. He knew nothing of women; they had not crossed so much as the very threshold of his life.

"You will soon be in flames," said White Crow, sneering again. "There is danger in this, also," she went on; and, placing her bony hand under the soft chin of Red Wind, she forced up her face and pointed to the great blue eyes and to the lips, parted as though in fear.

"What danger?" asked Thunder Moon.

"You have lived all these years in my tepee," said White Crow, "and still you are a fool."

In the meantime, she placed a dish of meat before Red Wind, and then hurried from the tepee, as though fearing that she might be called upon for other services.

Thunder Moon reached forth his mighty hand and took up a braid of the hair gingerly.

"I see no danger in this," said he, simply. "And in no other Cheyenne maiden or man had I looked into blue eyes. But is there a wrong in the color? You, Rising Cloud, are a wise man and a chief, and the brother of a chief. Tell me if there is danger!"

The wind had been rising, and now it increased heavily, and the patch of sun that fell through the opened flap of the tepee was darkened suddenly as though the sky had been overcast. Rising Cloud, before he answered, raised his head and seemed to listen to the storm. Then he looked down to Thunder Moon.

"Oh, my brother," said he, at last, "sometimes the trail cannot be followed by the sign, and sometimes the mind travels where words cannot go!"

Very often an Indian expresses himself in some such obscure fashion, letting his meaning be hinted at rather than spoken and defined. Most of the Cheyennes were experts in deciphering such hidden meanings, but the foster son of December ever was dull at this exercise of the wits. Now he shook his head and looked back to the girl.

"Tell me," he said, "in what manner Walking Horse has found evil and trouble in you?"

She looked down and sighed meekly.

"My father never has loved me!" she said. "Who can tell why? Evil spirits surely stand between me and him!"

It seemed to Thunder Moon that from the corner of his eye he saw his prisoner smiling, but he could not be sure.

"Eat!" said he.

"I am not hungry," said she.

"Have you had food today?"

"No."

"Then you are hungry."

She lifted her large eyes to him. They were filled with tears.

"Fear and hunger are not brothers, oh, Thunder Moon!" she said.

"Are you afraid?"

"I have been brought like a dog and flung into the lodge of a man who does not want me," said she. "I am among strange people, and my heart turns to water!"

Thunder Moon flashed a glance over his shoulder as though daring danger to approach. Then he said, "I have not said that you are not welcome here. You are very welcome! No danger shall come near you. As for White Crow, she is so old that she is losing her wits! Now eat. I myself, Thunder Moon, tell you not to be afraid."

She began to eat obediently, and every time she raised her fingers to her lips, her eyes went up, childlike, and rested for a moment upon the stern face of her new master, as though asking for further permission.

Thunder Moon began to smile a little, and nodded continually. He was on the verge of pointing out choice morsels, as a squaw does for her child. It seemed to him that Rising Cloud also was smiling, continually, faintly, though whenever Thunder Moon looked fairly at him, the Pawnee's face was grave enough. Something was wrong, he felt; but what it could be he was unable to guess, and before long he discovered that he did not care.

"Thunder Moon is happy," said the Pawnee suddenly.

"Yes," said the warrior, but corrected himself to add, "sad, also, my friend."

"Your tepee is filled with treasure, a beautiful woman has been given to you. Why should you be sad, Thunder Moon?"

The maiden ceased eating so that she might listen.

"I am sad, Rising Cloud, when I think that such a girl, young, beautiful and good, could be hated by her own father. That is what makes my heart heavy!"

The maiden continued her meal.

Now shouting and confusion began to come upon the village. The wind had increased to hurricane dimensions; clouds of dust began to invade the tepee of Big Hard Face, and now and again a lodge went down with a crash before the cuffing of the storm.

Thunder Moon went to the flap of the lodge and watched the vast masses of the storm mist hurtling across the whole face of the heavens, and saw the frightened Indians working furiously to make fast their lodges.

Big Hard Face came hastily into the lodge, pressing past his foster son unceremoniously.

"The Wind Spirits are angered, child!" said he, as he passed. "I shall make medicine. Come and help me! Where is White Crow?"

December was as hard-headed as any man in the tribe, but, like all the rest, these disturbances of the sky troubled him; they were the direct manifestations of the power of an angered deity. To Thunder Moon, however, they had a different significance. Since that day in his youth when he had first conceived that the Sky People had taken him under their peculiar protection, all the phenomena of the air fascinated him. He had stared at the sky many an hour and, watching its changing lights and drifting clouds, he had felt as though he were looking into the mind of Tarawa. Now this thronging legion of the storm spirits seemed to him an army singing a canticle in praise of the Sky People, and he wanted to raise his voice to add to the tumult. He controlled himself, however, for he knew that it would have seemed to the rest of his people a mysterious sort of blasphemy.

Now he saw Spotted Bull, dressed in the hideous costume

of his profession, staggering against the wind and approaching as rapidly as he could, followed by half a dozen of the chief men of the Suhtai.

When he came nearer, Spotted Bull turned suddenly into the lodge of December, crying, "Make way, Thunder Moon! This storm is of your raising. You have brought evil into this camp, and unless I drive it out, the Sky People will tear up all our lodges, and then tear up the Suhtai, also, and send us whirling away through the air forever!"

Saying this, he pressed past the warrior and entered the lodge with his companions at his heels, and the instant he was inside, he stretched out his arm toward Red Wind.

"It is in her!" cried Spotted Bull. "The evil is in her, and Thunder Moon had brought her into his lodge!"

"Drive her out!" shouted Gray Eagle. "Drive her out at once from the town! My lodge is staggering. Soon it will go down. The tepees of Snake-that-talks and Two White Feathers have been snatched away into the air! Drive her out at once!"

White Crow caught the girl by the arm and tugged at her.

"Get up, witch!" she shrieked. "Get up and go!"

Thunder Moon strode suddenly between his foster aunt and the girl.

"You are all fools!" said he. "I have shown you once within a day that Spotted Bull is a fool and a coward. The Sky People are angry. But not at us. Only, they are shaking our town a little as they rush away toward the mountains."

Spotted Bull, his face dark with malignity, stared at the youth and quivered with rage, but presently he shouted, "I will show you what my power is, Thunder Moon. I will show you that I could wither you up like a leaf, if I chose. But I pity you. Now I shall not drive this woman away. But I shall purify her, and presently the Sky People will make the sky clean again above our heads."

Thunder crashed at that instant, and such a terrible lightning bolt leaped down the sky that through the seams and the cracks of the tent it cast a bright flicker of light on those inside. With a groan, they cowered toward the earth—all save Thunder Moon and the girl, who kept her eyes fixed upon his face, as though half bewitched by his calm courage.

"Make haste, Spotted Bull!" cried December. "Make haste! I feel the Sky People pluck at the top of my lodge. The earth trembles. In another moment all of us will be whirled away."

CHAPTER

13

Thunder Moon, at this entreaty, at least relented in so much that he stood back a little, merely saying to the girl, "Do not be afraid. Spotted Bull dares not harm you. He is a fool; I have proved it before; and now he will prove it himself by trying to stop this storm! That will be the end of him!"

So said the warrior, sneering at the medicine man. The latter, in fact, understood his position perfectly well. The disastrous inaccuracy of his late prophecies, which had been meant to depress the influence of Thunder Moon had, instead, reared the fame of the young brave like a temple built of massive ashlar. For lesser failures than these, medicine men had been put to death as though they were dogs; and had not Thunder Moon possessed singular gentleness of spirit for a Cheyenne, the fatal blow certainly would have fallen upon the false doctor when the hero returned to camp with his prisoner. Even as it was, Spotted Bull was in a perilous position. His power had melted away. And, accordingly, he had seized upon the opportunity the storm gave him of proclaiming the vengeance of the spirits upon Thunder Moon. No matter how much the chiefs might doubt the power of Spotted Bull's medicine, they were too frightened not to listen to him with attention and watch for possible results. And so, by the springing of a sudden trap, as it were, the medicine man found himself committed to the desperate task of banishing the storm itself from the sky!

He fell to work, however, with a perfect fury, dancing wildly around the Omissis girl, who stood with her hands clasped and her head bowed, staring at the ground in quiet submission. Perhaps the passion of Spotted Bull was bipartite, partly assumed in a frenzy of fear, and in one portion really composed of a mysterious confidence that he was in touch with the spirits of the upper air.

The necklace of bear claws leaped and rattled upon his neck; his headdress waved and nodded madly; and all the time he kept up a prodigious racket by beating a rattle he held in one hand against a drum he held in the other.

In the meantime, he shouted forth in a chant, confused words of Delphic import; and only paused once or twice to throw a handful of sweet grass upon the fire, the smoke of which rose with the prevailing current of the air and covered the form of Red Wind with fragrant mist. Through that, Spotted Bull was seen still leaping and gesticulating, until finally he paused and struck an imposing attitude before the maiden and shouted, "Spirits of storm and terror, I see you. I have forced you to come down. Like a white eagle your king sits on the head of this girl. I see you. I name you. I command you to be gone! Be gone! Be gone!"

The only answer to Spotted Bull was a vast peal of thunder, and then again a perfect torrent of lightning flooding down the sky.

"See!" laughed Thunder Moon. "He is ten times a fool!"

The others could not see, however. Fear crushed their bodies and their hearts against the ground. Only the medicine man, Thunder Moon, and the girl remained erect, while Big Hard Face called hopelessly, "Kill Spotted Bull! He only angers the spirits! He will have us all destroyed!"

Spotted Bull apparently saw death literally rubbing elbows with him and he bellowed out, "Yell and shout, evil winds!

Pour down your fires! You are angry, because I am your master. The Sky People will hear me. They will herd you out of the sky like buffalo before the hunters! Go! Go! Go!''

So shouted the medicine man, and the prostrate, frightened Suhtai closed their ears and shut their eyes, expecting another roar of heavenly artillery.

Presently it came, but at an amazing distance; and, with a sudden inspiration, Spotted Bull rushed to the flap of the lodge and tore it open. There he stood, pointing above him with an arm stiffened by excitement, and shrieked, "Now, come to see! I have been heard. The storm runs away. Be gone, black clouds! I command you! Fall down the slope of the sky! Let the sun shine once more! Sun, shine down upon us! Let your rays tell the Suhtai that Spotted Bull has good medicine—has great medicine—that he can command even the winds, and he holds the lightning even in his bare hands!''

So screamed Spotted Bull, and the people in the tent hurried to the open flap and stared up to the sky; and there they saw—most miraculous!—that the deep masses of the clouds had parted and rolled away to either side, and now, even as the medicine man spoke, the shadows were parted from before the face of the sun and all the golden tide of his brilliance streamed once again over the earth. At that, as the wind fell suddenly away, a great song of rejoicing rose from the entire village, but it was as nothing compared with the excitement in the tepee of Big Hard Face.

He himself, though he was a thrifty soul, picked up a fine new rifle and thrust it into the hands of the great medicine man; and all the others followed suit by presenting gifts of some sort or promising others when they could get them.

By this lucky stroke, Spotted Bull had swept into the forgotten past the little matter of his false prophecy concerning Thunder Moon and the war trail. Nothing succeeds like success, and particularly like the success of today as against whatever may have happened yesterday. He filled the whole eye of the Cheyennes at that moment, for partly he was a hero for having defied the evil spirits of the storm and dared their wrath in person; partly he was a divine medicine man.

And his own joy was as tremendous as his fear and his despair had been great only a few moments before. Literally staggering, so dizzy was his head with his glory, he turned on Big Hard Face and said, "The maiden is purified. Now she cannot harm our tribe. As for that young man"—and here he pointed carelessly toward the famous Thunder Moon—"you have seen that I could have poured a river of lightning upon him if I chose. But I am merciful. I remember that he is young and that he lives in the tepee of a good friend, December! So I am merciful!"

He left, surrounded by the chiefs, and Big Hard Face hurried after him to join the chorus of praise.

There remained in the lodge the Pawnee, just recovering from sheer terror, Thunder Moon, and the girl. She had not stirred from her graceful position, and Thunder Moon, staring at her, half thought that he saw the drifting smoke of the sweet grass form above her head in the dim outline of an eagle!

He thrust the superstitious fancy from his mind.

"Is it ended?" asked the girl.

He nodded.

"And may I move?"

"You may. You are free to go where you will, Red Wind. The young men will show you my horses. And of all that is in this tepee you may make your choice. Of the rifles and the ammunition. Do as you will with them. I shall not force you to remain here."

"Ah," said the girl, "do you drive me out, also?"

"I?" cried Thunder Moon. "No but you ask me if you are free to move, and I tell you that you are as free as the lightning in the sky. Go where you will!"

"Where could I go? I am homeless in the world!" said she, and sighed deeply.

"You forget, Thunder Moon," broke in the dry voice of the young Pawnee. "You have given your word to keep this maiden."

Thunder Moon, recovering from his enthusiasm, bit his lip and darted an angry glance at the prisoner. But the latter was looking intently at the girl and apparently did not notice the wrath of his captor.

"In the middle of the storm," said Thunder Moon suddenly, "you were not frightened, Red Wind. While the rest—and even Rising Cloud, yonder—shrank and trembled, you were not afraid."

Her large, gentle eyes turned to him and dwelt upon him and his heart began to flutter with something like fear, though delight was blended mysteriously with it.

"You stood near me," said Red Wind. "I knew that you would protect me. The Sky People are like brothers to Thunder Moon. They never would step into his lodge!"

It made Thunder Moon fairly giddy, this speech, and he went slowly to the entrance to the lodge and paused there. His heart was beating at a prodigious rate. It was as though a vast opportunity had opened before him, and how to use it was not given him to understand. But he did know that the Pawnee was smiling again; knew it, though his back was turned to the captive.

Outside, the village was in an uproar. He could see a shouting crowd gather around the proud form of Spotted Bull, who was making a speech, in which he doubtless had much to say about his familiarity with the spirits, and in which he congratulated the Suhtai on having such a person as himself among them! Thunder Moon smiled a little in turn, a grim smile; and then he looked back to the girl.

She no longer seemed an Omissis maiden in the tepee of Big Hard Face, chief of the Suhtai. But the last smoke of the sweet grass clung to the ground about her feet, and a wisp of it shrouded her faintly, and the red-gold of her hair shone through. And to Thunder Moon she was of a more than earthly beauty.

He wanted to speak; words would not come; he was dizzier than before; and he stepped out into the open air and looked up to the blue of the sky from which the storm had been brushed away so oddly. He had no faith in the astral pretensions of the medicine man, but in spite of himself he could not help feeling that there was danger indeed in the presence of the Omissis girl.

CHAPTER

14

Big Hard Face was a man of practical mind, and he quickly recovered from the shocks of that day's events—the presentation of the treasure, the coming of the girl, the mystery of the storm, and the big medicine that had banished it. He reverted to the subject of the stolen horses and went to his foster son to urge him out on the trail. He found Thunder Moon like one in a trance, looking up to the sky that had given him inspiration so often but that failed him now, utterly.

"Then I ride myself!" said the old man hotly. "You have been bewitched and turned into a deaf stone and you are no longer a man, Thunder Moon!"

He would, in fact, have departed at once, with a chosen band of braves, had it not been for the arrival of a messenger who raced his pony through the village and flung himself down in front of Big Hard Face, gasping out a strange message. He had ridden out into the prairie, after the storm, to help locate the horses that might have been driven astray by the fury of the wind; and, venturing far out, suddenly a Pawnee riding a tall chestnut horse barred his return to the village and covered him with a rifle. Boy though he was, and armed only with a knife, he would have fought for life and scalp; but the Pawnee offered him peace and good will and merely bade him go into the village and carry word to Big Hard Face and particularly to Thunder Moon that the Pawnees were ready to bury the hatchet and welcome peace, if Thunder Moon would set free Rising Cloud. In return, the Pawnees would return all the ponies they had captured during the raid; and, particularly, as an assurance of good faith, they engaged to send in immediately, upon an appointed signal, the five chestnuts that had been stolen the day before. The Pawnees would give up the chestnuts merely as a signal of their desire for peace; but first they must be assured that their messenger would receive no harm at the hands of the Suhtai.

To such a proposal as this, there could be only one answer. The appointed smoke signal was sent up at once; and the wailing of the squaws, which was rising from all quarters of the camp in dreary assonance, ceased, and the curious mob began to assemble to see the Pawnee come in.

What a roar rose from the outskirts of the town when the Pawnee came! It swept closer. Big Hard Face was discovered in close and eager conference with his son. He was entreating Thunder Moon to listen to reason and agree to deliver up the captured Pawnee. For there was only a definite value to be attached to all things—even to such a splendid exploit as that of Thunder Moon in the Pawnee camp. But the foster son of the chief was gloomily silent. Only his eyes flashed when through the opening gap in the crowd of the Suhtai he saw a warrior, with the cropped head of a Pawnee, mounted on a spirited pinto, and leading behind him the five beautiful chestnuts that had been stolen from his father's herd.

Coming up to the lodge of Big Hard Face, in front of which that chieftain stood, the newcomer dismounted and saluted the Suhtai with much dignity, regardless of the savage hatred of the squaws, who were pushing forward eagerly, anxious to have clearer sight of this man who had some hand, doubtless, in the slaying of the lost Suhtai. But before the messenger could speak, a young warrior cried out in a thrilling voice, "Beware! It is Falling Stone himself! It is the new war chief of the Pawnees!"

That startling suggestion reduced even the squaws to silence. All, in a hushed reverence that was almost fear, pressed closer to stare at the victorious leader who had struck them such a dreadful blow. There was little about him to suggest that he might be the brother of the handsome and graceful brave, Rising Cloud. Lowbrowed, with wide cheekbones and heavy, brutal jaw, he looked like the lowest type of Plains Indian. But his eye was bright and clear; and when he spoke, one felt, instantly, the presence of a reasoning and keen intelligence. Moreover, though his body was scarcely more beautiful than his face, it was framed on such massive lines of strength that even Thunder Moon scanned the figure of the leader with something like apprehension. And all the striking and gripping muscles along his arms and in his mighty hands grew taut, as though he were stepping into combat with that chieftain at once.

Falling Stone said simply, "The son of my father and my mother is in the tepee of Thunder Moon; the lodge and the heart of my father are empty; I have come to ask for Rising Cloud; give him to me, oh, Suhtai; and take in exchange my friendship, and these horses as a pledge of it."

"My friend," answered Big Hard Face, looking intently at the other, "you have taken away many of my young men and you have brought us much sorrow. But every man must do his own work, and the work of a Pawnee and a Suhtai cannot be the same. I am willing to talk to you about setting your brother free. You offer five horses. It is very well. But that is not the price of your brother, I believe."

"I offer all the ponies you lost when I was last in this camp," replied the Pawnee.

"And how many is that, Falling Stone?"

"You, yourself can count them, my father."

"We have counted our losses. Three hundred and fifty horses that were grazed by our young men have been lost."

"They are not in my hands, however," replied the other. "But I shall give more than three hundred."

"It is not in my heart to make a close bargain," said Big

Hard Face, with pretended generosity. "Let it all be as you choose. Send me the three hundred ponies, and you shall have your brother—"

"If it is my will," broke in Thunder Moon sternly.

"In the camp of the Pawnees," replied Falling Stone, with cunning rebuke implied, "when one speaks to the father, one is also speaking to the son."

"True, true!" said Big Hard Face, speaking hastily and apparently out of the ebullient good nature that was in him. "Let it be as—"

"Father," said Thunder Moon, "I must be heard. But let us go into the lodge. The children and the women listen to us. It is better to speak to a few than to many."

"It is true," said Big Hard Face. "There are no brains in a crowd. It has no head."

And he ushered them into his lodge with much dignity. So the Pawnee brothers stood face to face again, and it was curious to watch their behavior.

Undoubtedly, in their own home, they would have rushed into one another's arms; but here they were before strangers, and they gave one another only a glance and a quiet word. The contrast between them was sharper than before; the war chief looked more abysmally brutish; the prisoner seemed more wonderfully graceful and capable of swift movement. One was a mastiff and the other a greyhound.

"Here in a Suhtai lodge, and living, I never expected to find you," said Falling Stone.

His brother answered in a soft and rapid voice, "I woke up with the knife of that man at my throat; he asked if I were the leader of the war party. Should I have said no, brother?"

Falling Stone cast a sharp glance of inquiry at Thunder Moon, who replied with equal brevity, "He gave himself to me in your place. I looked at both of you. But when your eyes were closed in sleep, I could not guess that you were the leader."

Falling Stone cast one eloquent glance of affection toward his brother and then was silent, waiting, with courtly majesty and composure. Thunder Moon said abruptly, "You have brought back to us five horses as a pledge of good faith.

Well, I shall buy back those horses. There are rifles in that heap, as you may see for yourself. They are not common horses; I offer you no common price. Take five rifles for each!"

The eyes of the war chief glistened, and Big Hard Face broke in, "Boy you put lightning in the hands of one who will pour it on your own head!"

"I have made the offer," said Thunder Moon, frowning at the interruption.

"It is taken!" said the chief. "The horses are yours again. And these are mine!"

He could not avoid picking up one of the rifles, and he put it down with the lingering touch of one who loved the weapons. Perhaps already he was imagining a score of his best followers mounted on good horses, and equipped with these new and first-rate guns.

"I take the rifles," said he, "and give back the horses. I accept the price you offer. Does that deprive me of the right to buy back the freedom of my brother?"

"No," said Big Hard Face eagerly. "The fifty horses—"

"Father," interrupted Thunder Moon, "I have offered a great price and bought back your horses. Now I talk of a thing that is purely mine—not mine, but belonging to the Sky People. That is Rising Cloud. The white spirit of the moon and the Sky People led me into the Pawnee camp. They made my feet silent even in the dead grass. They used my hand to kill three men. They gave me a chief as a captive. They carried me out of the camp again; and they sheltered me when I escaped, putting a mist over the eyes of my enemies. I offered them a sacrifice. A great sacrifice. Now I swear it! Rising Cloud must die to do them honor!"

The prisoner was silent, but a deep groan was wrung from the throat of his brother. Then there was a slight flash of light and Thunder Moon saw that it was the Omissis girl, turning gravely toward the captive; and in this light her hair was like the red of cornelian, shot with gold. But her eyes said nothing, and her face was like a mask.

"We two shall meet!" cried Falling Stone in a fury of grief and of hate; while Big Hard Face, thinking of the fifty lost

horses, covered his head and withdrew from the conference—
a mute recognition that his authority over his foster son had
reached a sharply defined limit.

"Let us meet, then," answered Thunder Moon instantly.
"Let us take out your brother, still bound, into the prairie
beyond the village. There you and I shall fight for him. He
who wins takes him!"

"Is it agreed?" asked the Pawnee eagerly.

"No," broke in Rising Cloud. "Listen to me, my brother.
You are great in war. But this man fights with a strange
medicine. The spirits point his guns. With that one, which
has six bullets, he knocks down the rabbits as they run. If you
fight with him, you die! I have seen him! I understand!"

Falling Stone, writhing with shame and with anxious grief,
cried out, "And you, brother?"

"As for me," said Rising Cloud, with the calm of a true
eclectic who had considered many forms of life and thought
and found them all light things, "as for me, I die with no
dishonor and shall be buried without shame. Thunder Moon
has given me that promise! But you—go back to our people.
You cannot struggle against the medicine of this pale-faced
Cheyenne. But do not forget me. And when you lead out
your war bands, let the braves shout my name when they
charge. Many Suhtai shall die for my sake."

It was no mere blazon of indifference the captive showed,
but a true resignation, and his brother looked long and
earnestly upon him.

"No man will believe that I have refused to fight for your
sake, Rising Cloud," said he. "But I am a naked warrior,
and Thunder Moon is shielded by the spirits. Only the Sky
People could have led him into our camp through all the
warriors. Do you forgive me if I ride away?"

"I forgive you with all my heart," said the prisoner.
"Farewell!"

Falling Stone went slowly from the tepee; as he passed out,
Thunder Moon stepped softly after him.

"I shall leave my guns behind me," said he. "Let us ride
out with shield and spear and knife only, my friend. If you go
back to your people with your brother, and with the scalp of

Thunder Moon, you will be the greatest hero who ever rode into the city of the Pawnees!''

Falling Stone regarded him with an odd mixture of hate and fear and wonder.

''Is it only a bullet that a spirit can guide straight?'' said he. ''I live and fight by the strength of my hand; I leave medicine to the medicine makers; say no more, for I shall not fight with you unless I see you in the middle of battle. Then be sure that I shall not go backward!''

So the guns were loaded upon the pony he rode, and Falling Stone departed slowly from the camp, riding with bowed head.

Had Thunder Moon been a true Indian, he could not have helped pushing his advantage and, to shame the Pawnee, riding after him and taunting him loudly on his way through the camp. But he was not a true Indian. As a matter of fact, he felt a certain degree of sympathy with Falling Stone, for Thunder Moon himself believed that his great deeds in war were produced more by a singular diablerie with which the Sky People had endowed him than by his native strength of hand and of spirit. But his heart began to rise. Now that the five lost steeds had been returned and paid for out of the price of the maiden it seemed that a crown of good fortune had been placed upon the head of Thunder Moon. Only one thing remained for him to do, and that was to return to the Sky People the reward he had promised them. Many sacrifices he had offered them. Many sacrifices he had offered before, but never a human life.

He went back into his lodge.

''The time has come, Rising Cloud,'' said he. ''Stand up, and come with me!''

CHAPTER

15

If in many ways Thunder Moon fell short of the wild cruelty of which an Indian was capable, yet it is equally true that no Indian ever could have sacrificed a human life with the calm of spirit that now possessed the warrior. To him, it was a spiritual rather than a physical act, and by many dexter signs he was convinced of the kindness of the spirit world and felt that he must make this great return to the Sky People.

The Pawnee, without a word, stood up and prepared to go with him; they had crossed halfway through the tepee when the soft, gentle voice of the Omissis girl said, "Oh, Thunder Moon, why do you sacrifice now, when the Sky People are far up in the heavens, living in the light of the sun where it is brightest and hottest? Do not give this man to the moon spirit or the sky; but wait until the dawn of tomorrow has filled the sky with rosy light; for then the Sky People are so close that we can hear the whispering of their feathers as they pass by."

There is an ecumenical rule that he who proceeds calmly to action by calmness may be dissuaded. So it was now. The passionate man is the hasty man, but there was no passion in

Thunder Moon, now. He hesitated, and then he smiled at the girl.

"How much truth there is in you!" said he. "How much wisdom! And yet you are a woman, and you are not old! And when I look at you, Red Wind, I feel that I am rich. There is no man among the Cheyennes who is so rich as I am in having you."

So saying, he gave up his purpose of the immediate sacrifice, and went hastily out from the tent. After the storm, all the prairie was fresh. The ground was soft. The horses would be running wildly and gaily. The children would be dancing and singing and tumbling one over another. And there was something in the heart of the warrior that sympathized with all this physical activity and made him, as it were, a part of all that he looked upon. But, crouching by the lodge entrance, he passed White Crow, and she stopped him with one of her keen, cruel glances.

"She is yours, but she is not really yours. You have not married her, Thunder Moon!"

He stopped, frowning. "What keeps you back?" asked the crone in her snarling voice.

Thunder Moon began to think aloud, purposely looking away from the ugly face of the old squaw.

"Now that she is in the lodge, she is mine to look at and listen to. But if I ask her to marry me—"

"You do not have to ask. She is yours to be taken!"

"I never could do that. For all I know, she may have a lover among the Omissis."

"Would you give her up, if she begged you to set her free and let her go to another man?"

Thunder Moon was silent. His forehead glistened.

And with the edged tool of her tongue she wounded him again.

"But if I ask her to marry me," went on Thunder Moon, boggling his words rather badly, "perhaps she will say that she does not wish to live in my lodge. Then what? Could I keep her? She would scorn me. I could not endure that. No, it is better to keep her as she is. For a while!"

The hag began to laugh, showing her pale, withered gums in the ecstasy of her mirth.

"I shall tell you what really is in your mind."

"Tell me, then," he asked, diligently avoiding her with his eyes.

A boy playing with the cascabel of a rattlesnake went by them, and the eyes of the crone followed him for a moment before she spoke again.

"I shall tell you, Thunder Moon. The spirits speak to you, do they not? They guide you?"

"Sometimes they do, when I pray to them."

"And sometimes when you do not pray! What spirits did you know to pray to when you were first a boy in this camp? But still, you lived! Well, the spirits speak in you. And those spirits now say to you, 'Leave that woman alone! Do not go near her. She is dangerous!' "

"How could she be dangerous to me, White Crow?"

"You do not fear her because she has given you no warning. But I tell you a thing: A rattlesnake makes a noise before it strikes. But a woman makes no noise. She smiles before she stabs you!"

Thunder Moon drew himself up in a sort of diaconal stiffness and dignity, saying, "You are too old to remember the mind of a pure girl. Do not talk to me any more about her! Mind your pots of meat and make the buffalo robes, and keep your thoughts away from important matters."

Thus spoke Thunder Moon, terrible in his surety and in his pride, and the old hag simply answered, "Does she make you happy?"

Her foster nephew said nothing.

"Well," said she, "let me tell you that one day she will bring you much more grief than all of the sorrow that is in the hearts of those wailing squaws!"

For the mourners had withdrawn from the camp. By the river, or on hummocks of ground nearby in the prairie, they were rasing their laments; and their voices came out of the distance mingled and softened but deep with meaning. The gates of the heart of Thunder Moon were opened and he felt that he was hearing the diapason of life, its fundamental harmony of sorrow and of despair.

"Never a wolf has made a kill," said Thunder Moon in a sudden passion of anger, "without the envious howl of a coyote close at hand. So it is with you. You have forgotten happiness. You would like to send it all out of the world?"

And he walked hastily away, deep in a mist of thought. Yet he could not go unnoticed. Whenever he stirred forth, a band of the striplings was sure to gather instantly around him; for at times, he was known to give much attention to them, telling them odd stories of his hunting and his fighting, talking more easily with them than with the men of the tribe. So they gathered about him, now, hopefully watching his face, and then trailing behind. Perhaps—who could tell?—he even would let them handle his knife, which had drunk the blood of so many enemies, or even fire his revolver. For he had done it before. So a little legion attended him whenever he walked abroad, running ahead, pulling from his path a dog or a little child that happened to be in his way, and even shouting to the women and to the warriors, "Step out of the way, there, and be quick about it! Thunder Moon is coming!"

The women, of course, scattered willingly and quickly enough. For, one and all, they were in deadly terror of a medicine man; and Thunder Moon was surrounded in part by the dignity of a warrior and in part by the efferent mystery that was breathed out around a medicine man and worker in wizardry.

The warriors moved more slowly from his way, grudging his greatness, but afraid of him, also. And so he went through the little village like a sort of superior being. But certainly by his passing he did not edify the morals of his compeers, but left behind him a trail of envy and wrath and subdued but fierce malice. So it is always with the great ones of the world. And the danger of Thunder Moon was all the more poignant because in his absentminded course of living he never dreamed what wild jealousies sprang up around him! And who was there to tell him of the truth? No one, perhaps, except White Crow; and by the continual gloom of her forebodings she had caused herself to be disregarded in her tepee almost as completely as another Cassandra.

Down to the river went Thunder Moon and sat on a stump and regarded the darkly swirling waters. He picked up a stone and idly he cast it into the stream. Instantly, half a dozen flashing bodies leaped from the bank and dived; the victor emerged with the stone in his hand and laid it with a smile of pleasure at the feet of Thunder Moon; then he stepped back and waited for a word of commendation—a glistening, slender young statue of red copper.

At length, the warrior looked up, and saw the children; he saw the dripping boy; he saw the wet stone at his feet. And suddenly Thunder Moon sighed. Someday he would like to have sons like these—slender, swift-footed, bright-eyed. He suddenly sprang to his feet. He would marry Red Wind, come of it what might!

And so he started back toward the village, and as he went the unending wails of the mourners sang a dreary monody in his ears.

CHAPTER

16

His little legion followed him. They were used to his absent-minded ways and therefore they did not show their disappointment, but escorted him through the town as they had escorted him out of it, clearing the way before him; and dispersing at last when he came to his lodge.

Thunder Moon went straight in and found Red Wind braiding her hair, while White Crow snarled softly to herself in a corner of the tepee, sewing beads upon a pair of moccasins, and the captive as ever sat erect, at ease, his eyes a blank.

"Red Wind," said Thunder Moon, "I have come to say a solemn thing to you!"

She looked up to him and saw in his face such pure emotion as might have served for song by the verge of old Castalia, and her fingers froze in the solid, metal masses of her braids.

"Master," she said, "I hear you."

"I have given my oath to keep you in my lodge; let me keep you as my wife!"

Her great blue eyes dwelt upon him as though in fear. Slowly her fingers resumed the thoughtless work of braiding the hair.

"Of all the Cheyennes you are the greatest and the richest," said she. "And I am only your slave. It is pity that makes you speak to me like this. But wait until the morning when you offer a life to the Sky People. Ask them then if you should do this thing. Then your will must be my will!"

She had not repelled him, and yet he felt the repulsion; and out of the distance he heard again the drifting, melancholy music of the mourning women. And from the side of the tepee he saw the evil grin of White Crow as she bent over her work. Then it occurred to him, suddenly, that no other Cheyenne would have spoken of such a thing to a maiden before listeners. He was shamed, and in his shame he withdrew from the girl. And like a shadow of prophetic spirit he saw dimly before him a shaping and forecasting of trouble.

Gradually, thereafter, it seemed to him more and more clear that he should have approached her in a different manner; but still he was reasonably certain that all would eventually go well, for as he looked at himself as at a picture, he could not help seeing that he was all that the girl had said: the greatest and the richest man among the Cheyennes!

The thought comforted him. And that night, as he sat in his couch and smoked before sleeping, he watched the others go to bed one by one, dropping the end curtain of soft antelope skins that shut off each compartment from the sight of the central portion of the tepee. The prisoner, first of all, retired for the night. Then Big Hard Face, then White Crow went to sleep, and soon the loud snoring of December rattled through the lodge. Last of all, the curtain dropped before Red Wind, and Thunder Moon sat for a long time looking at the dying fire that still shot up a red hand now and again and thrust wild shadows through the tepee. He felt that he was approaching a permanence in his life. He felt that he was secure of all the future. And in that security he lay down at last and slept in turn.

Physically he had done nothing the day before; but spiritually he had exhausted himself; and he did not waken until the full rose of the dawn was already in the sky; did not waken until the rough hand of Big Hard Face shook him, and the voice of the chief shouted, "Up! Up! They are gone! They are gone! White Crow, send out the alarm! Send out the searchers!"

Thunder Moon leaped up, reaching for a rifle.

"Who are gone?"

"Both! She must have set the Pawnee free. She and Rising Cloud have gone off together..."

What she? He did not have to ask that. But gripping at the center pole of the lodge and holding hard, he made his brain clear from the shock, made himself look back into the past. He could remember, now, that there had been many exchanges of glances between the two. And yet how marvelous that a woman's heart should be taken and given in silence! And to a helpless prisoner! But might it not be that his very helplessness had been the vital point of appeal to the girl?

White Crow was screeching with ugly laughter.

"I told you that the trouble would come! Now it is here, and you look sicker than an aching stomach and a bad tooth."

He reached out and caught her. He wanted to kill her. "Woman, devil!" he gasped at her, and stepped from the tent. Others were rushing out of every lodge entrance, gaping, chattering, and pointing toward him. Did he see smiles among them?

So he raised his head and stared around at them slowly, meeting eyes, and the smiles went out and then shrank before him—children, women, and proved, hardened warriors. They shrank under his eye, and afterward they would hate him for it. That he knew, but nothing mattered!

He flung a saddle on one of the chestnuts that stood beside the tepee, a glorious stallion, swift as the wind. Petted and pampered all its life, it nuzzled at his shoulder fondly, now, with pricking ears; but he struck it away with a brutal blow.

"Call me a devil if you wish," said the hard voice of White Crow behind him, "but do not make a fool of yourself and bring back a woman who detests you! She will only leave you again, or simply deceive you without leaving. This is the price, my son, of manhood!"

He listened, and looked up. The sky was brighter and more

beautiful than ever before, but not for him. Only where it arched above the head of Red Wind was there beauty in it, and all the rest of the world was a draped and solemn catafalque, where dead things and dead men lay. He gathered the reins; still he delayed to leap on the back of the horse. For perhaps White Crow was right, and this was the price of manhood, paid down in pain.

PART

TWO

CHAPTER

17

Thunder Moon looked wildly around him, striving to find some object that would win his mind away from his own torment. But he found none. All that he looked on seemed detestable to him. The lodge behind him—there was none larger or finer in the tribe—had seemed a place spacious enough for a man's ambitions to expand to the full. Now it was contracted to a miserable tent set in a huddle of wretched tepees, peopled with fools and savages.

Then he heard Big Hard Face arguing with White Crow inside the tepee. It was true, admitted Big Hard Face, that the woman would make more trouble if Thunder Moon brought her back to the lodge; but still, whether she would or not, his foster son was pledged to the father of the girl to keep her in his tepee. Find her he must, if he could.

That seemed to solve the riddle. Act he must, or else his whole soul would be dissolved in pain. And so he flung himself into the saddle. In the scabbard running beneath his right leg was his rifle. And in saddle holsters were two heavy Colts. At his belt was his knife, but now he called for his shield and his lance and White Crow brought them, mumbling protests still. But when she saw him grasp them, and sling the shield upon his back and brandish his spear, her eyes lighted with admiration. He was far from beautiful of face, but his sunbrowned body was so alive with power, and his seat upon the stallion was so sure and easy, that she felt him to be the very beau ideal of the Indian warrior.

So felt the others who watched him ride forth. Instantly the legion of boys swept around him, every one of them mounted on the fleetest pony he could beg from his father's herd.

"Take pity on me, Thunder Moon!" they begged in shrill voices. "Take pity on me and let me ride with you. I shall fight like a man for you. And you will have all the glory. Only let me go with you! I shall make the fires and cook and hunt for you. I shall find the trail for you. Take pity on me, Thunder Moon!"

So they rushed and swerved before him, each intent to show the skill he possessed as a horseman, and each brandishing a weapon of some sort. But while all the rest swept back and forth, striving to catch his eye, the son of Three Bears drifted just behind him, saying nothing, as one who resolved that if favors were to be granted he would be close at hand, but feeling that a boon so great should not be clamored for.

Not only did the boys beset Thunder Moon, but the finest young warriors among the Suhtai galloped up to him, having snatched their accouterments and hurried toward this chance for fame. Fame there must be, for Thunder Moon never had taken the war trail in vain. And, like a lion, he counted no coups, he took no scalps, but left these glories for those who accompanied him. And the young warriors were not alone; here and there Thunder Moon would see some grim-faced, tried man of battle, raising an arm in dignified salutation: "How!" Not begging to be included in the expedition, but manifestly hungry to be invited.

They came, in this fashion, to the edge of the village, and Thunder Moon looked back with a solemn and sad face, very much like one who turns to take a last look at a home he never may see again. So, turning and gazing, he encountered the bright eyes of the son of Three Bears, waiting, speaking not at all, but quivering under the glance of Thunder Moon as a swift horse quivers at the touch of the whip.

The heart of the warrior was touched. But he pointed to the pony the boy mounted. "Do you wish to go with me, and on such a horse?" he asked.

The question and the almost implied invitation in it made the youngster mute for an instant; then he cried out, "Let me come, Thunder Moon! You will see that this horse is not beautiful, but he will not fail me, and I shall not fail you!"

There was a sharp chorus of derision from the envious. The sons of rich men in the tribe swept in short circles, displaying the matchless feet of their ponies. "Take me, Thunder Moon! Take me! The son of Three Bears is mounted on a dog, not on a horse!"

"Have you asked your father's permission?" said Thunder Moon, noticing that the boy made no reply to these taunts, but kept his wild, bright eyes fixed upon the face of the man he worshiped, as though confident that, regardless of the words of the others, this brave could make no fault of judgment.

"I have not asked, but his permission is given!" cried the youth.

"There stands his tepee. Come with me."

He rode before the lodge. And out of it, as though a premonition of the question had come to him, stepped Three Bears and his single squaw. There was no more celebrated chief among the Suhtai than this man, and when all the ten tribes of the Cheyenne were gathered and their chief men in council, few were listened to more eagerly than this distinguished brave. In spite of wealth and fame, he had taken one squaw only; and by her he had one son—this child who now sought to take the warpath with Thunder Moon. The instant that they saw their son with the pale-faced brave, they understood the meaning; and the squaw ran to her boy with a cry and tried to pull him down from his pony chattering furiously in protest.

The father, however, smiled, and pretended to be happy.

"This is a great honor," said the chief. "I could not hope

that my boy, who is yet without a name, may be taken on the warpath by such a chief as Thunder Moon.''

The latter was too deeply buried in gloom to pay any heed to the compliment. He merely said, ''You are not like the tumbleweed, which scatters a thousand seeds. You have only one son. Will you let him go out with me on the trail? There will be danger, Three Bears!''

''Look!'' cried the squaw in a broken voice. ''You have all the boys and the young men of the Suhtai to choose from. Leave me my son!''

''I want no other than this one,'' said Thunder Moon. ''Of all the Suhtai he has the sharpest eye and the quickest ear, he is the swiftest on the land and the swiftest in the water, and he reads the sign of the trail as though it were picture writing on the wall of his father's tepee. Tell me, Three Bears, are you content that he should go with me?''

Three Bears cast a single glance at the face of his boy, and in that face he saw such a radiant fire of hope that he could only answer, ''I give him to you. Do what you will with him. If he can shoot straight when he comes home I shall be a happy man!''

There was a sharp wail from the squaw, but Three Bears, with a single rough word, sent her into the tepee, there to bury her fear and her sorrow.

And Thunder Moon said to the boy, ''Do you know the horses of my father?''

''I have herded them and watched them. I know every name and every trick they have.''

''Which is the most beautiful of all our horses?''

''Sun-path is the most beautiful.''

''Go to the lodge of Big Hard Face,'' said the warrior, ''and tell him then that you will have Sun-path. Take her; take also a good saddle and a bridle; take ammunition and also a rifle and one of these small guns that has six voices. Take all of these things, and a good knife. My father will give you all that you require. If you see a shield that is small enough, take the shield, also. And when you have what you want, ride rapidly out of the village and meet me by the waterfall—that one with the big linn beneath it.''

Having finished these instructions, he turned and rode instantly from the town. While he was still at a distance, he could hear the varying voices of the cataracts, some singing high, others ominously deep and low. He listened, and from far behind him he still heard the mourning cries of the Cheyenne women.

How clearly it seemed proved to Thunder Moon that there was little joy and much sadness in this bitter world!

Now he reached the fall that beat into the face of a large pool, and close to the verge of the water he sat down, and the big stallion came and stood close to him. Of all the horses of Big Hard Face, there was none like Sailing Hawk for strength or for endurance. And as he fled along the horizon line and over the hilltops, he had seemed often like a bird on the wing and won for himself his name. But the horse was unregarded, for Thunder Moon stared down into the pool and felt that all the future was as gloomy and dim as the surface of that broken water. He did not move until Sailing Hawk started and snorted softly. Then Thunder Moon turned his head, and across the plain he saw coming toward him the most perfect symbol and picture of wild, free grace that ever his eyes had beheld.

For yonder flew the son of Three Bears, riding the red mare by knee pressure alone, letting her reins fall loose, with both his slender arms extended exultantly above his head. Upon his left arm there was a small white-faced shield. In his right hand he held a lance, not of the massive proportions of that which Thunder Moon carried, but a slender-shafted weapon as fit for throwing as for thrusting in the charge.

His long hair flying back over his shoulders, the boy raced up to Thunder Moon, whipped from the back of the mare, and dropped lightly onto his feet, standing in the attitude of one ready to receive orders.

Thunder Moon regarded him with a faint smile. One thing was certain. Unless a Pawnee bullet tagged this lad, he would never be overtaken in any battles that might lie before them. Like a god of Speed incarnate was this youth.

And Thunder Moon, feeling old and gray before his time, pointed to a rock.

"Sit there," he commanded. "Before we take the trail, we must have council." He went on with such frankness as no Indian in the world would have used, above all to a boy: "I have lost a woman, as you know. My heart is very heavy because of her, and there is a mist on my mind. I do not think lightly and easily. Now, you must think for me. Consider, that somewhere in the plains all around us are a Pawnee and an Omissis girl mounted on two of the Comanche horses from my herd. In what direction they may have fled, I cannot tell. They had started many, many hours ago. I have wasted much time. These horses are faster and stronger than theirs, but how can we ride them down unless we know where the trail may lie? I have considered. My mind is all empty of wisdom. Now you consider, also, and let me know what to do!"

With that, he dropped his head on his hand and fell again into a brown study, watching the face of the water. As for the boy, his eyes glittered with joy at being thus appealed to. His own contemplation was not done with a bowed head and a knitted brow. Instead, he turned slowly to all the quarters of the horizon, looking fixedly in each direction. Then he dropped upon one knee, and on the ground he sketched what seemed a little map. He rose again, looked for a long moment to the southwest, and then leaped onto the back of Sun-path, and pointed the nose of the mare west and north.

"I am ready, master," said he.

"I knew that you would guess at something," said Thunder Moon. "Do we cast in that direction? Do you think it may be there that they have fled?"

"I do more than think," said the boy calmly. "I know that if we ride hard, when we reach the western edge of those hills in the middle of the afternoon, the two will not yet have come out onto the plain."

"You *know* that much? How do you know it? Well, keep your knowledge until we have met them! Ride first, to show the way. I am too blind for anything but fighting!"

CHAPTER

18

As they rode along, Thunder Moon gave his companion some vigorous lessons concerning first the mere holding of a rifle; and then its balance in the hands, and how to mark with the eye, before glancing through the sights; and how to find the bull's-eye by letting the uncertain farther sight wobble around the target until it found dead center; and how to aim a little low; and then, how to squeeze the trigger with a gradual pressure so that the explosion always would come with a bit of surprise even to the firer. He showed the boy all of these things, and how it was quite possible to do a very great deal of practicing without so much as discharging a gun. "For," said he, "you know whether your man is dead before the bullet reaches him; you know it by the way you held the gun on the mark."

The boy listened with an almost tremulous eagerness, and when Thunder Moon allowed him to practice—not with one bullet but with a whole score of rounds—the results his pupil achieved were totally amazing. As for the knife and the spear, he already could handle them with a sinister skill, and he could wield the shield and the lance together like a tried warrior.

So they prepared for war as they crossed the plains, but all the talk was not on the side of Thunder Moon. If he could teach in some respects, he could learn in others.

"Tell me," said he, "what sign you are following."

For his own eyes could detect no print on sand or in grass as they rode.

"No sign," replied the boy.

"Then," asked Thunder Moon a little sharply, "did you learn where to look for these two by medicine?"

"No," said the boy. "But where would they go when they left the camp? That was what I asked myself. And I stood and stared around at the edge of the sky. Shall I tell you what I thought of?"

"Yes, tell me everything."

"They would not leave until very late, after the last sounds had died in the town."

"That is true."

"And the squaws were crying until very late."

"Yes."

"Then, when these two slipped out from the camp, they had to steal two horses, and they took ones from your Comanche band."

"That is true."

"When at last they were on their horses, they were not like ordinary prisoners escaping. If they had been, they would have ridden straight back for the Pawnee town."

"And why would they not ride in that direction?"

"Because it was already late, and they knew that before long in the dawn light Thunder Moon would come rushing after them on his great tall horse, eating up the ground like a fire, so they were afraid, and they looked around them, I think, and said to themselves that quickly they must get off the face of the plains, so open—like the palm of a hand—and if they were seen, they would be destroyed. How could they escape from Thunder Moon, once his eyes found them?"

Thunder Moon looked at the boy seriously but he found no mockery in the eyes of the youngster.

"Then they saw," went on the youth, "the low line of the shadows to the north and the east, and they told themselves that first they would gallop straight for those hills, and pray to get to them before the morning light began. But after that, they would turn and ride around behind the hills, or through them toward the lodges of the Pawnees. This, I think, is the truth, and we should come to them not long after they leave the valleys of the hills and ride out into the open. May it be true! May Tarawa keep me from speaking a lie to you!"

He said it most fervently, and Thunder Moon, amazed by this exhibition of logic, was silent for a time.

"What is it that sees most quickly of all the things that run on the plains?"

"The antelope," answered the boy.

"What is it that hears most quickly?"

"The antelope also, when it pricks up its long ears and stands to listen."

"No ears are quicker than yours, and no eyes are sharper on the whole prairie," said Thunder Moon gravely, "for you see and hear partly with eyes and ears and partly with your own hidden mind. Therefore, I shall call you Standing Antelope, but never until you have counted coup on a Pawnee."

This threw the boy into an ecstasy, though as usual he controlled his emotion and said not a word, but for a long time afterward his eyes were glistening with pleasure.

They were passing now through a sea of grass, not very long, but growing thick and soft, an ideal fodder, and the buffalo were sure to know of such a rich pasture. In fact, little groups of them were seen here and there, the outlying members of some herd that wandered farther to the west.

The boy would have passed them by; his heart was bent on the great things to be done; but when they came upon a little swale, with a great bull standing in the center of it, Thunder Moon said, "Have you ever killed a bull?"

"I have killed one calf," said the boy regretfully, "and no more!"

"The rifle is loaded. Ride down into the hollow and kill that bull!"

One excited and grateful glance was flashed toward him,

and instantly Sun-path went flying into the swale toward the monster buffalo, like a red arrow from the string.

The bull, wheeling, made off at full gallop—for all his clumsiness, the buffalo can gallop at an amazing speed—but the red mare was alongside very quickly; the rifle was leveled, and fired, and at the single shot the bull dropped its head, turned a complete somersault and lay still.

Here was a thing worth narrating at the fire! What other boy of all the Cheyennes had slain a bull at a single stroke? The son of Three Bears was beside himself with joy, yet even then he remembered his manners and stood aside to let his elder dispose of the carcass. Thunder Moon, however, reined his stallion nearby and said simply, "It is your bull. Take what parts you wish. We shall have fresh meat tonight. You have done well; and remember that the bullet that kills a buffalo will kill a Pawnee also!"

So the boy took the tongue, and then with a knife expertly removed a few portions of the choice part of the haunch. They had not time to take the hide, of course. And in another moment they were swinging across the prairie again.

There was a difference, however. They had been man and boy, before; now they were like man and man, for the youngster had proved his weapon and confidence was in his heart.

It was late afternoon when they reached the edge of the hills on the western end of their range, and here Thunder Moon made a halt in the shadow of a rock ledge and loosed the cinches of the saddles so that the horses could breathe, while he and the boy lay among the upper rocks to watch. The sun was hot, but hotter than the sun was the heart of Thunder Moon as he stared over the waves of grassland and waited.

Even so, for all his eagerness, it was not he who had the first view of the quarry. The soft voice of the boy presently murmured, "Hai! They have come!"

Then he saw them; a gray horse and a brown, issuing from the shadows of the hills and striking at a trot into the open country. The girl was mounted on the brown; on the gray rode Rising Cloud, the Pawnee.

"They are mine!" said Thunder Moon in his savage heart of hearts, and instantly they returned to the horses, drew up the cinches, and rode out into the open lands.

Their horses had not made a dozen strides when they were sighted by the fugitives, and as pigeons scatter when the hawk flies toward them, so the girl turned and sped back toward the hills, while the Pawnee darted straight ahead.

First, Thunder Moon let his heart lead him, and swerved toward the girl; but then rage mastered him, and he pointed the head of the stallion at the gray horse of Rising Cloud.

CHAPTER

19

A stern chase is a proverbially long one at sea. By land it is not much shorter, if the course is laid upon the open prairie and the horses are in any degree fairly matched. But in this case they were not matched. Tough and true were all those Comanche ponies that Thunder Moon had stolen in the hot southland, but never for a moment could the striding of those shorter legs match the long gallop of the chestnuts. Like an eagle, with strong wing strokes, ran the stallion; like a rapid hawk beside him flew the mare, with the boy erect and joyous in the saddle; and with every moment the distance that separated the hunter and the hunted grew less and less.

Rising Cloud twice wheeled in the saddle and discharged his rifle at his pursuer. Well-aimed bullets they were, and as they were fired, Thunder Moon turned his head a little and regarded the boy. The son of Three Bears merely shouted with joy as he faced battle fire for the first time—laughed and shouted and urged the swift mare to greater efforts, until even Sailing Hawk, weighted as he was by the vastly heavier bulk of his rider, hardly could keep pace with the smaller horse.

The stolen pony on which the Pawnee rode, however, was beaten by superior speed, not mastered in endurance; and to the last stride he continued to fly across the prairie with head and tail straight as a string in the greatness of his effort.

Once more Rising Cloud slewed himself around in the saddle to take aim, and now they were at hardly more than half pistol shot. It would be madness to endure that point-blank discharge. So Thunder Moon snatched a revolver from its holster and fired quickly. The gun exploded in the hand of Rising Cloud, but the bullet sped at random and he swayed heavily to one side, reeled, and almost fell.

"He is gone!" screamed the son of Three Bears. "He is dying!"

And, giving wings to the mare, he closed in on the enemy with a burst of speed that threw him ahead of Thunder Moon. Rising Cloud had snatched up the lance with which, as well as with the fallen rifle, he had been equipped. Through his right shoulder the bullet of Thunder Moon had passed, and blood was spurting over that side of his body; but in his left hand he balanced the spear and thrust sharply with it at the Suhtai lad, at the same time swerving his pony to the side and shouting his war cry.

There was no trace of the craven in this Pawnee. He intended to die fighting gloriously. And his first stroke was toward the boy. The son of Three Bears dipped on the back of the mare and, striking up the weapon of the Pawnee, he pressed in and smote the half-naked body of Rising Cloud with his clenched fist.

"So I count coup! I count first coup. I count it!" screamed the boy, as the charge of the mare swept him past and out of the reach of danger.

But for that matter, Rising Cloud had a greater task on his hands than the defense needed against a boy. The most terrible warrior in all the hosts of the Cheyennes, those ferocious horsemen, now swept down upon him. When he saw that the Pawnee possessed no gun with which to fight but had to defend himself with the spear alone, Thunder Moon had thrust his revolver into the holster—the rifle he never had touched—and taking his lance he closed on the Pawnee. His own spear gripped in his unskillful left hand, the Pawnee could not withstand this attack for an instant. His weapon was beaten aside by a cunning of a lancecraft as great as a rapier parry, and then, dropping the spear, Thunder Moon grappled his foe with his bare hands.

The boy had swerved on the mare as rapidly as a bird on the wing, and rushing back with spear ready to thrust the Pawnee through and through, he withheld his hand with a shout when he saw Rising Cloud torn from his saddle and instantly mastered in the herculean grip of Thunder Moon.

Vainly the Pawnee brave writhed and struggled. His right arm hung helpless. And even had he possessed his full might of hand it seemed that he could not have fought against this giant for a moment.

Now, wounded and disarmed, Rising Cloud lay on the ground, and the Suhtai warrior had dropped on one knee beside him, knife poised.

He grasped the fallen brave by the scalp lock, and holding him thus securely, he looked up at the broad, bright sky above him, where the sunset color was just beginning.

"Sky People," he said, "if I give you this man as a sacrifice, be kind to me and teach me what to do with the woman."

He looked down at the Pawnee.

"Why should you kill me, Thunder Moon?" asked the victim.

"You have murdered the Suhtai; you have been sheltered in my lodge from the women who wanted to torment you; and then you have stolen a woman from me and ridden away with her! Are those reasons, Pawnee wolf?"

"The Suhtai I fought with were killed in the open field," answered the Pawnee. "You kept me from the hands of the squaws in your camp, and for that I thank you; and as for the woman, it is more true that she stole me away than that I stole her."

"That is a lie, and the gray father of lies!" said Thunder Moon.

"It is the truth," said the captive. "How could I have escaped if she had not cut the rope that held me fast? But she cut the rope and whispered to me to follow her. When we were outside, she gave me a gun and a lance and a knife. I told her that she had better go back into the lodge—"

"Even the snake that twists through the grass at least speaks truth when it speaks," said Thunder Moon, "but you are not honest. I think that you loved this girl of the Omissis, and you made her love you and stole away with her—"

"If I were the head chief of the Pawnees," said the captive, "then I should take her into my lodge, because there is no other woman in the prairies who is like her; but since I am not the head chief, I shall have nothing to do with her."

"That is a likely story," said Thunder Moon, with a sneer. "And when you were outside my lodge with her, you told her to go back?"

"I told her that one of us might escape from you, but that no woman could flee across the prairies as fast as you would pursue."

"But she would not listen to you? No? She loved you so much that she would have to go with you?"

"She did not love me, but she would rather have fled away with an owl or a buzzard than stay in your tepee and become your squaw."

At this, the knife quivered in the grip of Thunder Moon, but with an effort that made his neck muscles bulge, he held himself from striking.

CHAPTER

20

The Pawnee, in the meantime, regarded his captor gravely and steadily. Thunder Moon stood up and began to walk back and forth, full of his thoughts. Sometimes he paused, determined to slay the Pawnee at once in sacrifice to the Sky People; and then again he felt an overwhelming need to know the truth about Red Wind, and what she had said to her Pawnee companion.

So he said to the boy, "Help to stop the bleeding of his shoulder. Wash that wound and tie it so that it will bleed no more."

The wound was dressed with the rough and quick skill that all Indians possess in such matters. Then Thunder Moon came back to the captive, saying, "Tell me. What is Red Wind that she detests me? Where has she found a richer Indian? Who has killed more enemies? Who rides on swifter horses, or has a bigger herd? Who keeps more guns in his lodge, and who has such stacks of softest buffalo robes?"

"Can a woman marry a horse, a gun, or a buffalo robe?" replied the Pawnee.

"Pawnee coward! Creeping, sneaking skunk-bear!" cried Thunder Moon in a wild fury. "Do you dare to tell me that she answered you that way?"

"Why should I tell you any more?" asked Rising Cloud. "You call me by many evil names and you will not believe me. Besides, you are about to sacrifice me, to send my spirit up to attend the Sky People. Why should I talk before I die? No, you may go to Red Wind and ask her all of these same questions!"

"There are ways, however, of making men talk!" said Thunder Moon, with a crafty smile.

"There are ways," said the Pawnee, meeting the eye of his captor firmly, "but you will not use them."

"I shall not?" cried the Suhtai chief.

"Because you jump when you hear the cry of a child, and you will not so much as lift a scalp. You have no heart for torture, Thunder Moon!"

The big man glowered at his prisoner, but he said nothing for a moment. The Pawnee, in the meantime, sat composedly, cross-legged, on the prairie; his face already becoming grave and dignified like one about to receive his death and meet it in the best manner possible.

The son of Three Bears ventured to speak. His nostrils had flared wide and then contracted again.

"Why should Thunder Moon trouble himself with such work? Let Thunder Moon go away and ride on the prairie. When he comes back, he will find that this man will be ready to talk of anything that is asked!"

Thunder Moon waved him away.

"This is a man and not a sick coyote," said Thunder Moon. "And you could tear him to pieces by little bits, you could send birds to tear him, and devour him, but still he would not speak after he had once tightly locked his teeth!"

There was a glitter of pleasure in the eye of the Pawnee as he heard this compliment, spoken unwillingly, though it was.

"But your speech may be bought," suggested Thunder Moon.

"What price do you pay to a dead man?" asked the

Pawnee. "How many robes and guns and horses will you pay to a man before you sacrifice him?"

"I could kill you," said Thunder Moon, "by the hand of that boy and let him scalp you and take your medicine bag. So that your spirit would be doomed to dwindle and die like a whistle on the wind."

"It is true," said the Pawnee, his face unmoved, no matter what desolation was in his heart.

"But suppose that I promise you an honorable burial with your weapons beside you, and kill that horse so that your spirit may ride it in the other world? Is that a price that would make you talk?"

"What would make me sure that you would do these things?" asked the Pawnee anxiously.

"My honor and my promise," said Thunder Moon.

"We have made many treaties and had many promises from the Cheyennes," said the Pawnee darkly, "and what has become of them? They went away in the wind like dust!"

Thunder Moon drew himself up.

"I am not a boy," said he. "And I have not spent my life in my lodge, like a woman. I have spoken in the council. Also, I have ridden on the warpath. And when has Thunder Moon failed to make his word good?"

The Pawnee reflected.

"That is true," he admitted at last.

Silence fell between them.

"It is a great price," said Thunder Moon suddenly, "to pay in order to know what words a woman spoke. But I will pay one still higher. I remember that you have sat in my lodge and eaten meat from the meat pot and slept there; your voice has been heard in my tepee. Therefore I cannot hate you, Rising Cloud. You are a Pawnee, but I think that you are a good man. Some day I may meet you in the battle at the side of your brother. Then perhaps the Sky People will give me strength to kill you both. But in the meantime I shall give you your life, and that rifle to carry back to your people, and that horse, so that you may go back not as a beggar but as a warrior who has escaped with honor from a great danger. Now, if that price seems enough to you, tell me everything that passed between you and the woman, and leave out nothing!''

The Pawnee was schooled, like all Indians, to control his emotions stiffly when in the presence of strangers; above all, he knew how to guard himself when he was with an enemy. But now he could not help a quick exclamation of wonder. He looked at Thunder Moon; he looked past that hero to the boy and saw the son of Three Bears writhing with rage and disappointment.

''You have spoken!'' said the Pawnee.

''The Sky People may hear me!'' said Thunder Moon.

''That is not necessary,'' replied the Pawnee. ''For it is true that all men know the honor of Thunder Moon is not the honor of a wolf or a snake. Now, I shall tell you everything. When I sat in your tent and the woman was brought in by her father, I looked at her and saw that she was beautiful. I have seen many young women in many tribes, but none like her. I thought that her father was anxious to get rid of her because she was wicked. Why else should he send her away and pay such a great price to the man who would take her into his tepee even without making her his wife? So I thought that perhaps I might be able to talk to her and make her my friend and then escape through her. I looked at her when I could; I smiled at her. But it was like smiling at the painted bear on your father's lodge. She would not see me. So I was a great deal surprised when in the darkness of last night she came to me and cut the rope that tied me. We went softly outside the lodge and she gave me the weapons, as I told you. And then, as I have said, I urged her to stay at the lodge, because she could not escape with me. But she would not stay. And she gave me a reason for it.''

''What reason, then?'' asked Thunder Moon.

''She said that you are a paleface, and that therefore someday you will go back to your tribe, and Tarawa would pour sorrow on the heart of any Indian maiden who married you.''

''Pawnee,'' said Thunder Moon sternly, ''it is true that my skin is not so dark as yours; but still it is not white. Some men are dark and some are light. Snake-that-talks is almost black, but who says that he is not a Cheyenne? As for me, no one but a fool and the son of a fool would think that I am not a Suhtai. I am the son of Big Hard Face. Is not he a Suhtai? Have I not been known these many years as a Cheyenne? Or is my life a dream?''

"I hear you and I understand you," said the Pawnee, in rather a gentle voice, "but I know that I have seen white men at the trading forts. Some of them are very white. Some are brown from living in the sun. You are like those brown ones. You are not like a Suhtai in your looks or in your ways; you are not like any Pawnee, or like any Sioux or Comanche that I have seen. So I believed the woman when she told me these things. She did not want to stay in your lodge and become your squaw.''

Thunder Moon bowed his head. He felt more crushed with sorrow than if he had been told of the death of a good friend.

"I could not persuade her to stay there," went on the Pawnee. "I asked her what she wanted to do, and if she would be a squaw to me when she came to the Pawnees. But she said that she did not want that. She only wanted me to help her get away. Afterward, she would think what she would do. When I heard this, I talked no more. It was dangerous to crouch there in the dark, talking. So I went with her to the place where your Comanche horses were. We stole two of them. We led them a little way off. Then we put on them the saddles that we had taken from your tepee. We rode away. And I cannot tell how you found our trail, unless the Sky People sent a spirit to sit on your shoulder and tell you how to ride!''

Thunder Moon looked at the boy. There was triumph in the eye of the latter, but no boast upon his lips.

"It is the son of Three Bears who read your mind," said the warrior. "All that passes on the prairies he sees. All the sounds that come down the wind he hears. He is like the standing antelope. And that is his name. When you go back to your people, tell them that the Suhtai have a new warrior, who is young but very wise. And his name is Standing Antelope.''

"I shall remember him," said the Pawnee, his eyes narrowing

a little with menace and malice. "Now, Thunder Moon, am I free?"

"You are free. Take the horse and all that you carried away from my tent. Go back to your people, Rising Cloud."

The latter, in silence, secured the Comanche pony, sprang on its back, and then darted off at full gallop. He did not pass straight away, however, but swung around in a short circle and came back before Thunder Moon.

"Listen to me," said the Pawnee. "Spotted Bull is no friend of yours. But he has spoken the truth. There is bad medicine in Red Wind. Leave her trail. Let her go and disappear in the prairie like a small cloud when it rises in the sky on a very bright and hot day. She will bring no happiness into your tepee!"

"Tell me," said Thunder Moon. "What have you learned that makes you sure of all of these things?"

"How does one learn about the eagle?" asked the Pawnee brave. "By watching it fly! How does one learn of the mountain lion? By following its tracks. And that is how I have learned about her. No man ever can be happy with her."

"I am not blind," said Thunder Moon. "Already I have sat in the same tepee with her. But I see nothing wrong about her. My mind is filled with mist when I hear you say these things. I cannot tell why her father wanted to send her away from his lodge. Why should he hate her?"

The Pawnee listened, frowning in thought.

At length he said, "I shall tell you only one thing. Her father does not hate her. No, no! But he is terribly afraid of her. That is why he sent her away, because he saw that if she remained in his lodge much longer, he could not remain the head chief of the Omissis."

"You answer one riddle by telling me another!" said Thunder Moon. "What do you mean by this? Why cannot he remain the head chief of the Omissis if she remains in his lodge?"

"I have given you my last answer," said the Pawnee. "My arm swells and the fever will begin soon, and I have a long distance to ride. Farewell, brother. Bad fortune may come to you and yet you never will lose two friends among the Pawnees!"

With this he wheeled his horse again, and this time he did not return, but headed across the vast prairie, when he soon diminished almost to a point that seemed to waver up and down with the heat lines that rose from the surface of the plains.

CHAPTER

21

Thunder Moon, after watching the retreating brave for a moment, turned to the newly named warrior at his side, and the boy cried eagerly to him, "You have given life to that lying Pawnee. You have kept your promise! Now, let me ride after him. He has only one arm. But he is older and stronger than I am. Let me try to catch him. It will be my first scalp, and I may count coup on him again!"

"I cannot give a thing and take back my gift again," said Thunder Moon, smiling a little. "He could not escape from you. His pony is fast and tough, but Sun-path is tougher and stronger. She would be up with him in a very short time, of course, and then you would have no trouble in killing a man who has not a bit of strength in his wise right hand. Tell me, Standing Antelope, is there any glory in killing a helpless man?"

"Why is there not?" asked the boy.

"Begin on the back trail that will lead us to the Omissis girl," said Thunder Moon. "But now as we go, tell me what

glory comes from destroying a man who cannot fight back
against you?''

They rode side by side through the grass, swinging at a
swift gallop toward that rift in the hills into which the girl had
disappeared when she turned back from the Pawnee who had
accompanied her.

"Are the Pawnees our friends or our enemies?" asked the
youth in counterquestion.

"They are our enemies," admitted Thunder Moon, smiling
at the idea that they might be any other thing.

"Well," went on Standing Antelope, thinking hard as he
rode, "if they are enemies, then every wounded brave someday will be healthy and strong again, and then he will ride out
to kill us. And for all of those reasons, my father, we must
kill the Pawnees, young or old or sick, and take their scalps,
and count coups upon them!''

Thunder Moon said nothing. He had learned from bitter
experience, even in the lodge of Big Hard Face, that his
thoughts were not the thoughts of his tribe, just as his
strength was not theirs, and their strength was not his.

He was silent for another and far graver reason; and that
was because he wanted to turn in his mind the words the
Omissis girl had spoken to the Pawnee. She had called
Thunder Moon himself a white man! And for that reason she
did not want to remain in his lodge!

The blood of Thunder Moon grew hot with anger.

As for a trifling matter of lightness in color, what was that?
Very gladly would he have had his skin a copper red. But
since that could not be, he was certain that in his heart he was
a good Suhtai, devoted to the interests of the tribe.

And as for being a white man—a *white* man!

Indeed, from hot his blood ran cold. He had had glimpses
of those people. Strangely, stiffly dressed, unless they attempted
an awkward imitation of Indian freedom of costume, they
moved out onto the prairie, trading for furs, quarreling with
one another, making cunning bargains, cheating their custom-
ers, deceitful in their councils, and only worth attention
because—so the wisest chiefs said—behind these white people there was a mysterious power, and in their hands there

was medicine of strange strength, so that sometimes ten of them, standing shoulder to shoulder, might beat off a hundred Indian enemies. But, place one white man in the plains, and even an Indian boy like Standing Antelope could account for him and bring in his scalp before many days of trailing had ended.

Such was the white man—such was his meaning to Thunder Moon. No wonder that his lip curled with scorn and with disgust when he heard that the Omissis girl had placed him in the category of these strange, unpleasant creatures! No wonder, also, that the girl, thinking such thoughts of him, should wish to leave his tepee, even with a man she found a captive there. She had fled away as from a curse. But now he wanted with a tenfold desire to find her, let her know the error of her thoughts, and so bring her happily back to his lodge.

Afterward, he would see to it that his skin should be darkened with certain stains of which he knew. Yes, he would make himself a figure of flaming red, if necessary, so that foolish thoughts might not come into the mind of the spectator— into the mind of Red Wind, above all!

So he pushed forward vigorously, and Sailing Hawk answered with a mighty stride that devoured the ground before them.

They entered the shadowed mouth of the valley into which the girl had gone; but instead of going straight up the hollow, young Standing Antelope—transfigured even in the eyes of Thunder Moon by the name he now wore and by the coup he had so lately counted—rode up to the top of the left-hand ridge, swung down from it and crossed hastily to the opposite height, and then with a wild war cry raced straight down the ridge and toward the open plains beyond.

Thunder Moon followed, thinking that the boy must be mad, but as he gained the mouth of the valley, he saw the brown pony racing sturdily over the plain, and the girl jockeying her mount along with a skill that no brave could have surpassed.

He shook his head as he loosed the reins of Sailing Hawk. How like a fox she was! For his own part, he would have pushed deep into the hills on her trail; and when he finally solved the trail problem, it would have led him back to the prairies onto which she had doubled.

He could thank Standing Antelope for this day's work, and in his heart he vowed that instant that he would make the lad a present of all the weapons he carried on that day.

So he sent Sailing Hawk after the fugitive.

She rode well; but she rode not well enough; and young Standing Antelope rode well also, but he could not rival the wild speed with which the stallion now plunged ahead, inspired by his rider. Past Standing Antelope went Thunder Moon, as though the boy were standing indeed; and the girl drew back to him. It seemed that the short-legged pony was laboring upon a treadmill, so swiftly did the stallion overtake it, and Thunder Moon, as he drew near, saw the girl turn her frightened head and glance back.

Exultation filled him. His war cry burst from his lips. His shadow fell upon her. And the next instant he had swept her from the saddle!

CHAPTER

22

So slender and so graceful had she seemed on the horse, so delicately light, that as Thunder Moon reached for her he half felt that the power of his grip would crush her. But behold! It was like grappling with a muscular man. Tense and swift she whirled upon him and a knife flashed in her hand and hovered at his throat. With desperate speed he clutched the knife hand, and the weapon fell from her numbed fingers.

Sailing Hawk came to a halt, and Thunder Moon let his captive drop lightly to her feet.

Standing Antelope galloped the mare behind the girl and remained stiffly alert in the saddle, spear in hand.

"Do not trust her, my father!" said he. "I saw her try her teeth on you. Tarawa made her hand slow or else she would have murdered you; and then I should have had to kill her. She-wolf! Little mountain lion! Remember that I am standing here behind you!"

Thunder Moon dismounted slowly and then waved the boy aside.

"Go catch the pony," said he to his ally. "And then keep away for a little. I wish to talk."

So Standing Antelope withdrew, and as he rode away toward the Comanche pony, he kept his head turned and watched this odd pair—the man so massive in his power, the girl so slenderly made, but with her dauntless head flung up.

It could not be said that she was merely hostile. She was more or less than that. Rather, she looked at Thunder Moon with fear mixed with some other emotion he could not understand.

He touched his throat, where the flesh still tingled as though the knife had pricked him there.

"Red Wind," he said gravely, "do you know what is done among the Suhtai when a woman takes a weapon and turns it against her man?"

She was silent.

"She is tied to a post of the lodge and then she is whipped until her back bleeds."

The girl did not wince.

"And afterward?" she asked.

"And afterward she is turned loose and thrust from the village with her feet bare and no food and no weapon to save herself and made to wander across the plains until she dies, or until she finds some wandering group of warriors who will take her off with them if they see fit."

"Turn me free, then, without a horse or weapon or moccasins," said the girl, "and whip me first until the blood runs down my back."

Thunder Moon winced.

"That would be easier for you," he suggested bitterly, "than to return to my lodge with me?"

Words may be bullets, at times, but silence is a pointed gun, full of awful suggestion. She was silent again.

"I understand you," said Thunder Moon, the blood rushing hot into his face. "You would rather be left to starve than come back with me. I am like a sick dog to you, hateful when I am near you."

She kept her large, grave eyes upon him and still said nothing. And he wondered at her, for her expression was perfectly masked, and not the slightest shadow of feeling appeared there.

In the other days, when she first came to the Suhtai, he had felt that her features were too immobile. But when she had swerved upon him as he seized on her today, he had changed his mind. Never had fear or despair been more eloquently shown than they were shown then in her face.

"All is well," said Thunder Moon sadly and angrily. "You would knife me like a Pawnee. Yes, you would kill me far sooner than you would kill a Pawnee."

A new thought came into his mind and startled him.

"But why was it," said he, "that when you had snatched your knife, and when my hands were busied with the reins and with holding your body, why was it then that you did not drive home the knife in my throat?"

There was a change in her, then. A sudden start, and a sort of shadow that fled across her eyes. It was gone at once, but he knew that in some manner he had disturbed her composure.

"I understand, however," he went on, as the explanation came to him, "and the truth is that you would have plunged the knife into my body, except that you knew that afterward there would be a terrible accounting with Standing Antelope. Tell the truth. Be brave and tell me that this is the truth!"

She merely watched him, calmly, without expression; and Thunder Moon felt reproved when not a single sharp word had been spoken to him.

"Mount your horse!" he said, pointing to the pony that Standing Antelope, in the meantime, had captured and brought back to them. "Mount your horse, and be sure that, for my part, I would not trouble to bring you back to the lodge of my father. I would not wish to keep you, but would let you wander over the prairie wheresoever you might choose. Only, my promise to your father holds me. Do you believe that?"

"No," said the girl.

And the monosyllable unbalanced his strength of self-content. He looked at her more narrowly. Yet she did not speak with the edged tongue of an insolent woman, seeking for an opportunity to inflict pain. Rather, she was watching him with thought, and filled with quiet contemplation.

Thunder Moon felt his easy strength ebb from him. He was about to slip back into the common resource of all men who feel themselves weakening and fly into a fit of temper, when a soft puff of wind came over the prairie, making the grass flash under its feet, and bringing to the warrior a delicate fragrance. That wind, as it were, blew through his soul, and carried his anger away with it.

So he let the girl mount without any reproof from him and he, in turn, leaped into the saddle on Sailing Hawk. Then he waved the girl ahead, and he followed with Standing Antelope. His anger began to return again, for why should the girl have been so sure that he had another reason for bringing her back to his lodge? And what other reason, really, did he have? To take as his squaw an unwilling girl was a depth of cruelty and folly quite beneath him; and yet he felt that she was right. There was some other motive that impelled him; and to face the loss of Red Wind would have been harder than to see all his other goods in the world destroyed before his eyes.

"She does not sing sorrow," observed Standing Antelope, gravely approving of the erect carriage of the girl as she rode before them.

Thunder Moon made no answer. He was growing more and more irritable, and poor Sailing Hawk had to pay tollage for the troubled spirit of his master; for, as the stallion made a side leap in passing a small hole in the ground, Thunder Moon cut him shrewdly with his whip and then reined in the charger with wicked violence.

The boy observed and contained his disgust for a moment, but finally could stand it no longer.

"When a dog is beaten, there is a woman in the lodge," he quoted from folklore tales.

"Why do you say that?" asked Thunder Moon, turning his frown on his young companion.

"Because I see that you are angry," said the boy, "and I know that you cannot be angry with Sailing Hawk!"

The warrior said sternly, "You have done well today, Standing Antelope. You have hunted down a hard trail. You have brought me to the enemy. And you attacked him bravely.

You have a reward. You have counted a coup and won a name; and, beyond that, I give you the rifle and the revolver you carry and the knife, and the lance, and the saddle. Now you may ride out as a warrior. But more than all this, I give you strong advice, 'Do not speak before your elders until your opinion is asked.'"

Under this rebuke the boy winced, but he maintained his new dignity with rare determination, saying, "Oh, Thunder Moon, the word of a friend is better to me than the counting of twenty coups or a herd of a hundred horses! I cannot take these gifts from you!"

"Do I have to beg a child to take what I offer him?" exclaimed Thunder Moon, flying into a greater rage.

"You have offered me rich gifts," said the boy gently, "but you have taken away your kindness from me at the same time."

"It is true! It is true!" said Thunder Moon, recovering instantly from his fury. "I am like a sinew-shrunk old horse, and I stumble as I go. If I took my heart away from you, Standing Antelope, I give it to you again, and all the arms and the other gifts with it. I have lost my temper like an old squaw!"

Tears of joy stood in the eyes of Standing Antelope as the warrior made this confession, and his young breast heaved suddenly.

"You have taught me how to be a man," said the boy. "You have let me count my first coup on a man you had made helpless; and now you have filled my hands with weapons. No brave among the Suhtai will be so envied as Standing Antelope. But ah, my father, the rest is as nothing to me, now that all is well between us!"

CHAPTER

23

All through the day, the interest of Thunder Moon in this child had been growing, and now it increased with a sudden bound; and looking at the boy he knew that his was the high and pure strain of Indian blood that furnished the tribes with their great chiefs—great in war and great in council, not mere seekers for blood and scalps but leaders of their nations.

So he said to the boy, with a smile, "You are wise, Standing Antelope."

"Father," said Standing Antelope, "if I had been blind, still I could have told that the woman had angered you by your voice as you spoke to Sailing Hawk."

"How could you tell that?"

"I have heard you talk to him as if he were a man. All the Suhtai know how you go out into the pastures to visit him, and how he comes running when he sees you, and how he guards you through the herds of the horses. We have seen how he trembles for joy when you spring on his back. And the warriors say that even battle he loves less than he loves his master."

Thunder Moon, soothed by this speech, passed his hand along the shining neck of the stallion, and the big horse tipped his head a little to look back at his rider, and his step, which had been smooth before, became as light as the wind.

They had skirted the hills to the south; and now, voyaging over the plains, they came in sight of the distant lights of the village. For the evening had thickened about them as they journeyed. At the same time, they reached a little run of water and a group of low trees.

There Thunder Moon halted. He could have pressed on into the town at once, but for a reason he himself did not understand in the least, he wished to delay that return. They soon had a fire blazing—a fire of reckless height, for it might attract the attention of any prowling bands of horse thieves such as were forever wandering near the limits of the Cheyenne city. And in this fire the girl roasted the meat Standing Antelope gave her.

She accepted it without a word; without a word she cooked it; and when it was roasted to a turn, she gave all to the two men and retired a little.

The boy, starved by his day's work, instantly began to devour the roasted bits with avidity; but Thunder Moon ate more slowly. And suddenly he said, "Maiden, you also are hungry. Come nearer to the fire. Take the meat, and eat."

Standing Antelope exclaimed, "Is it fit for a woman to eat in the presence of warriors, father?"

"Then go sit by yourself in the dark," said Thunder Moon impatiently.

"He has spoken the truth," said the girl, as Standing Antelope, his dignity much outraged, picked up a portion of the meat and retired with it.

"Whatever he has spoken," said Thunder Moon, "it is my pleasure to have you come to the fire and eat."

She came closer to the fire and sat down, cross-legged. Yet still she was half in the darkness, and the massive, metal-red braids of her hair glistened in the firelight and seemed to reflect their own color upon the face of the girl.

"I am not hungry," said she.

He saw that her eyes were downward, upon the fire, and an

unreasonable anger came upon Thunder Moon. He seized the whip that lay beside him and with it struck the ground.

"Eat!" he commanded.

Without a word, she reached for a morsel of the meat and obeyed him. He forgot his own food and leaned forward to watch, for this simple action of hers filled him with a strange satisfaction.

Twice she stopped, and twice with a gesture he forced her to continue.

"Is that meat poison, Red Wind?" he asked her at length.

Instead of answering, she merely lifted her head and looked steadfastly at him, and he stared in return, looking deeply into her eyes. Even by firelight, the intense, rich blue of them was apparent to him, like water under a deep sky.

"Tell me, Red Wind," he asked again, "why it is that you speak to other men and tell them lies about me?"

He was tremendously irritated when she refused to answer him, merely continuing her grave observance of his face.

"Why is it," he went on, "that you stole out with the Pawnee wolf, Rising Cloud, and told him such a lie as this: that I am not an Indian at all, but a white man? How could you find such a lie in your heart?"

"Is it a lie?" she asked him in her quiet voice.

And the simple question shocked all the blood from his heart to his head and made his face burn.

"Am I like one of those cringing, sneaking people?" he asked. "Am I like a mangy coyote, which dares not eat until after the wolf has left the prey?"

"Are the white men like that?" she returned.

"Are they not? What do they have except what the red people leave for them on the plains? How do they live except by the wealth of the Cheyennes and the others who ride on the plains?"

She waited a moment, and then, as though she forced herself to speak, she said slowly, "I have been to two trading forts; I have talked with trappers and with soldiers. Some of them are bad men; but all of them are wise. They told me of great cities beyond the Father of Waters. They told me of cities so great that into one of them could be poured all of the tribes of the red men who ride on the plains.''

"Do you believe such lies?" he asked her, scornfully.

She went on, after another little pause, "They are so rich that in one of their cities are more wonderful things than all the prairies and all the thousands and thousands of buffalo. And they build canoes in which five hundred men sit, and those canoes are driven by fire, fast as a horse can run on the firm land, and also, over the land, they send wagons of fire that—''

"Red Wind," said the warrior, "I listen to you and I wish not to smile. I see that they have told you such lies as even children, among the Suhtai, would laugh at.''

"I also laughed," said the girl, "but then I went to the edge of the great river with my father, and up the stream through the night we saw lights coming, and there was a great roaring like many winds although the winds were still, and up the waters against the current where no Indian could drive a canoe, a monstrous boat came. It had many bright eyes that threw rays of light across the prairie; and all over the boat we saw people walking.''

Thunder Moon moistened his dry lips with the tip of his tongue. He lighted his pipe and first blew a breath toward the sky and then a breath toward the ground. After that he crouched on his heels and smoked slowly, contemplatively. Wild thoughts were quickly passing through his mind.

"I have heard you," said he at last. "I do not wish to believe that you say a thing that is not. But if they have such magic as this, why do not the white men drive the Indians from the prairie?''

"It is not magic. Medicine men do not make the fireboats. Medicine men do nothing among the white men. Only, they talk a great deal. But they do nothing else. With their hands, the white men make these things. And when they wish to take the prairies from us, then they will take them. An old man among the Omissis has told me so. I have seen the boat of fire. And I believe.''

"This is very well," said Thunder Moon. "No matter what the old man may have told you, since plainly we are the chosen people of Tarawa and never may be destroyed by the white men; but perhaps you did not altogether despise me when you said that I was a white man?''

She would not answer; again, leaving that very open opportunity for giving him a handsome compliment.

''At least,'' said Thunder Moon, ''tell me for what reason you called me a white man?''

''Can we tell a dog from a wolf?'' she asked him in return.

''Surely we can do that.''

''And by what tokens?'' asked the girl.

''The wolf has a looser skin; he has stronger jaws; he is more wise on the trail; he is more quick to flee; and he is more terrible in fight.''

''And if you see a dog with a loose skin, with powerful jaws, wise on the trail, quick to flee, but terrible in fight?''

''That would be no dog, but a wolf!''

''True,'' said the girl. ''So I see you, Thunder Moon, and I call you a white man, because you and all your ways are white!''

He listened like a man bereft of his wits.

''Is this the truth that you speak, and not a thing to merely anger me?'' he asked her.

''You are a great warrior,'' said she, ''and so are the white men, though you do not believe it. They count no coups and take no scalps; neither does Thunder Moon. You make no medicine. Neither do the white men. The white men make their squaws into men and their men into squaws. And so do you!''

She did not alter her voice as she delivered the last stinging sentence; and therefore it was a moment before Thunder Moon understood her meaning, and he turned a deep crimson, a furious, deep crimson.

''It is time to mount!'' he said hoarsely, and he started to his feet.

CHAPTER

24

He knew, as he climbed into the saddle, that he had not, even then, taken the true Cheyenne course with her. For most of the stalwart braves would have rewarded this final speech of Red Wind's by throwing a handful of dust into her face and then flogging her soundly.

However, all he could do as Standing Antelope put out the fire was to ride up to her and say grimly, "You speak evil of the whites; are your own eyes and your own hair black?"

The last ray from the fire illumined her face; it was utterly blank and the expression indecipherable. Yes, no matter what the color of skin, hair, and eyes, her heart was the heart of a true Cheyenne. He knew it, and her silence laid a load upon his heart. He wanted to answer; but she gave him no opportunity with her muteness.

So they journeyed on through the darkness; it was a double night to Thunder Moon. They entered the village, and instantly their coming was known. Boys and women flocked out from the tepees and rushed around Red Wind, screaming at her, and calling her vile names. For she had committed the last crime for a Cheyenne girl—she had fled with one of their most detested enemies. And one woman leaped up and caught Red Wind by the sleeve to drag her from the back of her pony. Once pulled down into the midst of those reaching hands, she would be scratched, beaten, torn, and disfigured for all her life. And Thunder Moon waited for her scream for help.

No scream came. She struck away the hands that gripped her. But three or four more vengeful squaws grappled with her, and Thunder Moon had to ride in among them and brush them away. They fell back before him, calling him a fool, begging him to let them work their revenge upon this traitor to her nation. But he promised them his whip across their faces if they rushed at the girl again.

So they rode through the camp, and when they were close to the lodge of Big Hard Face, they passed the tepee of Three Bears. That hero stood before the open flap of his home, illumined faintly by the firelight that flickered within. No doubt his heart was bursting with curiosity to learn all that had happened on this trail, but he remained with folded arms, immobile.

Thunder Moon drew rein, and he grimly noted that the girl, even if she were unwilling to appeal to him in the midst of danger, at least dared not to ride on without his protection. She turned her horse beside him.

"Three Bears," said the warrior, "I took your boy away with me. He had no name and the braves did not know him. I bring him back a man!"

There was a stifled cry from the squaw of Three Bears and a deep shout from the excited listeners who had pressed around; but Three Bears did not stir.

"The quickest eye and the truest ear belong to him," went on Thunder Moon, "therefore his name is Standing Antelope. The Pawnee was wily and cunning; but Standing Antelope was wiser by far. The Pawnee rode fast and well, but Standing Antelope rode faster. The Pawnee turned to fight for his life. His spear was in his hand. But Standing Antelope rushed in and counted his coup!"

A wild uproar of applause followed this statement.

Then silence followed, to hear the result of the fight.

"Why should we kill a wounded wolf? We sent Rising Cloud on to his people to let them know that before long we should come again and strike them, and leave the plains covered with their dead men and send their ghosts to die in the wind!

"So we come back to you. And if any man doubts that Standing Antelope is a warrior, let him look, and see that he carries a spear and a rifle and a revolver that speaks six words. With every one a man may die!"

The boy could endure the strain no longer, but flinging himself from his horse, he fell into the arms of his father. His mother clutched him then. Hubbub broke loose around them. And then Thunder Moon turned away with the girl toward his own tent. As he went, he could hear behind him a shrill, boyish voice chanting above the tumult, chanting the first of his war songs, telling how he, Standing Antelope, won the name of warrior, and counted his first coup upon the body of a Pawnee chief.

It gave Thunder Moon a certain solace in the midst of the darkness that was settling over his mind. So he dismounted and waved the girl before him into the lodge, where White Crow and Big Hard Face waited for them. The noise had apprised them of what to expect, and the tongue of the hag was well loosened for her work. She sprang up and hurled a torrent of insults at the head of the girl. And Red Wind, her hands clasped loosely before her endured the storm without a rejoinder.

"Stop her tongue," said Thunder Moon to his foster father.

"Be still," commanded December.

"It is only the beginning of her evil!" exclaimed the squaw. "Walking Horse gave us the price of fifty horses for keeping her. But she will do us harm to the value of a thousand horses before the wicked spirits come for her, like brothers for a sister."

Big Hard Face raised his hand, and White Crow relapsed into an angry mumbling.

Thunder Moon beckoned, and old December came out with him into the open night. They walked together without a word through the village, taking care to avoid all who were abroad. And that was not difficult, for behind them the first war song of Standing Antelope was gathering a crowd; and there the boys, mad with envy, went to hear him, and there the warriors gathered to encourage such deeds of valor in the youth of the tribe.

Out upon the prairie went the two, and reached the bank of the river and sat on a fallen log. Beneath them, the stream ran black and smooth, with the faces of the stars fallen in it like flecks of cold fire.

"And Rising Cloud?" asked December at last, as though they had discussed all other things except the fate of the Pawnee warrior.

"He was sent to his own people freely," said Thunder Moon. "I could not kill a helpless man."

Big Hard Face stifled an exclamation. "That mercy will cost many a Cheyenne scalp!" said he. "Do you think that there is gratitude or kindness among the Pawnee wolves?"

"I think nothing," said Thunder Moon. "I am very sick."

And stretching his arm around his foster father, he bowed his head on the shoulder of that venerable chief.

Who else of all the braves among the Suhtai would have been guilty of such weakness? But the heart of Big Hard Face swelled in him with pain and sorrow.

"All that is evil comes from woman," said Big Hard Face. "But all the harm that an old wise woman can do is nothing compared with the danger that lies in a beautiful girl. I shall tell you why Walking Horse sent her away instead of marrying her to a man among the Omissis. He is the foremost of all of their chiefs. His war raids have taken him from the Sioux to the Comanches; and when he was in the southland he took from the Comanches a woman they had captured in Mexico. He made her his squaw, and before she died, she gave him this daughter. When she grew older, every young man among the Omissis coveted her. They tied their horses at the lodge door of Walking Horse. They tied ten, twenty, thirty horses at the lodge post. But still the girl would not have any of them for a husband, and Walking Horse feared to give her away because if he married her to one warrior, she might smile on another, and that would mean war in the camp. And the braves began to hate Walking Horse, because they thought that he would not give the girl to them. Once a bullet sang past his head as he walked through his own camp. Twice, knives were drawn against him. Then he saw what he must do. He came to the Suhtai and settled among us, until he discovered the lodge where the strongest men dwelt. To that lodge he gave the girl. But, being an honest man, he gave a great price with her. But now I shall gather together the price which he paid down with her and take her and the treasure back to him.''

''No,'' said Thunder Moon.

His foster father was silent.

''She has found the way into your heart,'' said he. ''But do not take her for your squaw. She has soft hands. She will not make your lodge happy or fill it with robes she has dressed. There is no labor in her. Not words but work makes a good wife. I shall tell you about women. They have long hair but little wisdom; they are a trouble when they are with us, but we miss them when they are away. Only to make mischief they are wiser than men. Woman speaks best when she thinks least, for in all things she is the opposite of man. She is beautiful, but she is soon old. She is more filled with cunning than a coyote, and though you watch her, you cannot keep her from stealing from you. A man may lie gravely, but a woman lies with a smile. When she smiles, soon you will have to spend treasure. We think that we possess her; it is she who possesses us. So from these things, my son, you will see that it is much better to live without a wife. Or, if you have a woman in your lodge, let her be an old drudge and not really your squaw. But if you let a woman bear a child to you, then she never will have done until she has made you her slave. Therefore tell me, my son, that if this woman has stolen into your heart, you will put her out again straightway!''

''Father,'' said Thunder Moon, ''she hates me with all her heart; but I never shall be happy until she is my squaw!''

CHAPTER

25

Big Hard Face listened to the words of his foster son with interest but without speaking for some time.

Finally he said gravely, "When a man desires a thing greatly, there is a time when it is best to study not whether the thing is good or bad, but how it can be got; and now you wish to know whether or not you can win the love of this woman?"

"No," said Thunder Moon, raising his head, "for first of all I wish to ask you about the things she has said to me. You, December, are my father."

"It is true," answered the Cheyenne.

"Then how," said Thunder Moon, "can I be called a white man?"

Big Hard Face started violently.

Then, turning to Thunder Moon, he asked sharply, "Who has put that question in your mind?"

"What does it matter? The question is asked," replied the warrior.

"It is the Omissis girl," said the chief savagely. "Who

knows a child so well as the parent? But if I had guessed that such an evil spirit were in the girl, I never should have taken the price of the fifty horses from her father, when he came to us and begged us to take his daughter into our lodge!"

"This is a simple thing," replied Thunder Moon. "I have asked you a question, and all that is needed is for you to answer no! There is no drop of the false blood of a white man in your veins."

The chief considered for a moment.

"I have taught you that the white men are partly villains and partly fools, have I not?" he asked.

"You have taught me that," replied Thunder Moon. "But between me and the other braves of the Suhtai I feel that there is a difference, and Red Wind says that it is the difference between the red man and the white. And where the moccasin covers my foot, the skin is white!"

"It is better," said Big Hard Face, "to consider the chattering of prairie dogs at the entrance to their holes than to worry about the words of woman! We have talked enough, my son. Let us go home to the lodge and sleep."

The mightiest hand among all the Cheyennes was laid upon the shoulder of Big Hard Face.

"Wait a little," said Thunder Moon.

The chief listened, leaning forward slightly.

"You are sad," said Thunder Moon. "Why is that?"

"I am sad because when I was a young brave the warriors did not listen to the lying voices of the women!"

"The color of my skin says that the woman is right," replied Thunder Moon.

"It is because you wish it," answered the chief. "You wish to be one of those strange people. You wish to call yourself white, and to leave your people and go among the strangers!"

"Look!" said Thunder Moon.

He pointed. The moon was rising, and in the direction of its broad and golden horn he extended his arm.

"I see it," replied the chief.

"Would not a man be a fool to give his word in the presence of the Sky People when he wished to speak a lie?"

Big Hard Face was silent.

"Yet I promise you," said the warrior, "that it is not so much what the woman has said as it is something inside my heart that makes me ask you these questions. Open your heart to me. Admit at once that I am not like the rest of the Suhtai. Where they smile, I am sad. Where they are sad, I smile. Who is there among the Suhtai that does not shudder when Spotted Bull frowns? But I have no fear of his medicine. He cannot make the sky either pale or blue for all his medicine. Also, the ways of the Cheyenne upon the warpath are not my ways. The coups and the scalps they prize are not my prizes. And in everything we are different."

"Look at the horse herd," answered the chief with much warmth. "Though the dam and the sire are the same, what two colts are alike? One is a fool and a sluggard, and the other is as swift as the wind!"

"That is true. But men are not like horses. I run more swiftly but not so far as the Cheyennes. I am stronger in my hands. With a gun I am more sure. I cannot endure pain as they endure it. And every moment that I draw my breath I know that I am not like my brothers of the Suhtai."

"It is the woman who talks by your lips," answered Big Hard Face, grown sullen.

"It is not the woman. What other brave has killed as I have killed? When I ride out to the battle, the Pawnees divide before me; and the Comanches scream to one another; and ten men ride against me; but even all the ten shrink before they come close. The Sioux know me, and the Blackfeet run before my face. The Crows cry in their lodges for the dead men who have fallen before me. What other Suhtai has killed as I have killed or been such a power in battle? Or in the council, who makes the old men grow silent when he speaks? To whom do the old men listen? It is to me! Still, I am not a chief. And the young warriors say, 'He never endured the trial of pain. When his father would have pierced his breasts and tied the thongs in the flesh, he screamed and refused the test. His shame is before our eyes.' Therefore, December, it is plain that I am not like the others. Red Wind says that it is because I am a white man. You must tell me the truth, for I see that you are not speaking with all your mind to me!"

Big Hard Face started to his feet.

"I shall go back to my lodge," said he, "and take the woman and give her the whip across her shoulders. I shall make her admit before your face that she says the thing that is not true!"

"Do not touch her," said Thunder Moon. "You are no longer young. There is little power in your hands. Do not touch her!"

"Because you would fight me for her sake?" exclaimed the chief.

"I have not said it."

"I hear it in your voice!"

"Perhaps it is true!"

Big Hard Face flung his robe over his head.

"My own son raises his hand against me!" said he. "It is time for me to go out in the winter and let the wolves gather around me. I no longer am valued in my own lodge, and my son lifts his hand against me."

He turned away toward the village, but the great form of Thunder Moon strode before him.

"I have asked you many questions," he said. "The man who does not wish to answer finds many chances to fall into anger. And if you leave me now, I shall believe all that Red Wind has told me!"

Big Hard Face recoiled from him.

"Then what would you do?" he asked.

"Blood calls out to the heart of a man," said Thunder Moon. "I should go to my people and learn the ways of their speech!"

"Go, go!" cried December. "Go, and let us remain behind you with an empty lodge! For this I have raised you! For this I have been a father to you! Would your own mother have labored for you as White Crow has worked? Would your own father have given you such horses and such weapons?"

He checked himself as his tongue was about to run on, but already he had said far too much.

"Then it is true!" cried Thunder Moon in a broken voice. "All that Red Wind said is true, and I am not a son of the Cheyennes! Far off in a lodge of the white men, my father and my true mother mourn for me. In the winter they are hungry because I am not there to hunt for them. In the summer, the white braves scorn them because they are poor, and have to walk beside the dogs that drag their travois!''

"No, no!'' exclaimed Big Hard Face, waxing warm. "You speak like a fool! The home in which your father and mother live is greater than fifty lodges such as mine. And in their lands many fine horses are grazing. They are rich. All the wealth of the Suhtai is hardly equal to the wealth of your father and your mother!''

Thunder Moon was silent. And in the silence Big Hard Face came to realize that he had, indeed, spoken far too much. He gathered the robe closer about his head and started back toward the lights of the village, but his foster son did not follow him; and suddenly he returned to Thunder Moon and dropped his robe to the ground. The moon played upon his old body, heavy but still strong.

"Oh, Thunder Moon,'' said he, "what is it that you do? Do you renounce the Suhtai who have been your brothers? Do you give them up for a strange people? What is the color of the skin? It is the color of the heart that matters!''

"I am a Suhtai,'' said Thunder Moon gravely. "I am a Suhtai, and nothing shall make me have another self! I am a Suhtai, but now I see that I am a Suhtai only in my love and in my thoughts. In every other thing, I am a white man, and among the white men I belong. Like them, I must learn to live as a coyote lives, eating the carrion the wolves leave after their feasts on the buffalo they have pulled down.''

Big Hard Face reached out his hands and found those of his son. He gripped them hard.

"Now I part myself from the thing I have loved more than I have loved life!'' said he. "I part myself from what is best and dearest to me in the world. But out of wrong no right can grow, and I have done wrong, and therefore I must be punished. The Sky People who I thought loved me have treated me as a fool is treated. They have let me grow old before they showed that they hated me. Sit down, and I shall tell you everything as it came to pass!''

"You are tired and sick at heart,'' said Thunder Moon,

trembling with excitement. "Wait until tomorrow. Then we shall talk again about these matters."

"There is no tomorrow for me," answered Big Hard Face sadly. "What life has a childless man? And now I am childless! The women scream and cut their flesh for the sake of their dead sons. But I cannot scream and gash myself. For I have no son. All these days I have lived a lie. My tepee has been empty, even when I let Thunder Moon fill it with honor and with fame. I have no son; and the son that I had was only a sham and a pretense!"

CHAPTER

26

"What is an old man but an unhappy man?" said the chief to his foster son. "Age makes a man gray, but it does not make him happy. It is a sad guest in the lodge. Old age is like a smoking fire. And even though the greatest chief lives to the greatest age, still he must die at last. Is not this true?"

"Perhaps it is true," said Thunder Moon, taking pity on the manifest grief of his foster father.

"What is the cure, then, for age?" asked the chief.

"I cannot tell."

"Think, however."

"I cannot tell, for the same cure would be a cure for death, also."

"There is a cure for death, oh, Thunder Moon!"

"Then I cannot guess it, for the stoutest of the buffalo will grow old and die at last."

"Then I shall tell you. A father lives after death in his son. For when death puts an end to the swiftest and the longest race, still something may be left after. The bow may be grasped by another hand; the horse may be ridden by another warrior; the lodge may shelter another, and the same Tarawa to whom the father prayed will send fortune to the heir. It is in our children that we live again. And the hope of our children makes death a shadow that otherwise would be a terrible force and steal every moment of happiness from our lips. So I tell you these things, because as I speak to you, so it was with me. I was a great warrior. I had many horses. No lodge was greater than mine. In no tepee was there more meat. And all the wise men in the tribe listened when I spoke at the council. But as the time grew, I still had no squaw. Do you ask me why, Thunder Moon?''

The foster son held silence.

''Because my face is cursed with ugliness,'' said December. ''The women would not look at me. They turned away their faces when I was near them, and when I had gone by, I could hear them laughing. So I could not take a squaw who would give me a child. And as for women for their own sake, I never prized them. We cannot live except through another; but mothers are loved by their children only!

''So I grew older, and I looked around me and saw that a time would come when I would have great wealth, but there would be in my lodge no young man growing wise and strong to take in his hands the weapons that someday I would have to lay down. There would be no one to sit by me when I was ill, and there would be no one to catch my horse and saddle it when I grew weak. And the more I thought of these things, the sicker and the feebler of heart I became.

''At last I saw that I could have no happiness unless I did something to cure this evil. So I thought long and hard on that matter, and at last I determined on the thing to do. He who wants the fastest horse in the world cannot expect to find it in the next lodge, and if he does, another warrior says that it is his. So I decided that for the thing that I wanted I should ride to a great distance and try to find between the East and the West something that would be worth giving up my life for, some great action by which the Cheyenne nation might remember me, even if I grew old without an heir. So I crossed the dark of the night and the whiteness of the day many times; and I came to rivers, and followed some along the banks, and others I swam across with my horse, but still I came to nothing that seemed worth dying for. At last, I came to the land of the white men."

Here he paused, but though Thunder Moon now could guess what was coming, he said not a word.

"I journeyed a great distance among the lodges of the white men. They have tepees built of stone and of wood, and there were grass lands and fruit lands. There were many horses and cattle, and such richness that nothing in the world could have been worth it except the open freedom of the prairies. Never had I seen such things, and never have I dared to speak of them among the Suhtai, for fear that men would laugh at me."

"What things, then, did you see?" asked Thunder Moon in a hoarse voice.

"The trails that they traveled were made of rock broken and laid thick upon the ground. Ten thousand buffalo might run across them in the rainy season and never break their surfaces into mud!"

There was a grunt of wonder from the warrior.

"The smallest lodge that I looked at was so large that two or three of the finest tepees among the Suhtai could be put in it. All around their houses in the fields grow all the fruits and the corn that men could want for eating. They do not ride on the warpath. They may sit still at home and there they will have all that they wish. There is more wealth for one of those great lodges than for all the Suhtai nation!"

"Then it is true," said Thunder Moon, in amazement, "for now two tongues have said it!"

"At last," said the chief, "I came to a place of many great trees and I rode through fields, and there were no houses for a great distance. But at last I came to the greatest house that I had ever seen. It was so great that I trembled when I saw it. Smoke came from several places at its top. I thought surely that Tarawa must live there! I lay in the woods, moving slowly from place to place that day, watching the great house and wondering. And everywhere I saw men working in the fields, or coming back from the fields to little lodges built not far from the great one. Then I came to a pasture and in that pasture I saw the finest horses in the whole world. I took some of them. You know about them. They are the chestnuts that you yourself have ridden against every one of our enemies, and they have never failed you in battle or flight or hunting. I saw them standing in the field together, and I trembled again. 'These are the horses on whose backs Tarawa dashes across the skies,' I said to myself. But they were very gentle. When I came to them, they let me take them. They were like colts, too young to know what fear is. I took some of them and especially I took the great stallion, the king of the herd.

"Then I lay in the woods close to the house, waiting for the night to come before I started away. And as I lay there, I saw a woman come out from the house carrying with her a small white child, and she put the child down under a tree. I crept a little closer. I looked at that child. I thought that I would take a scalp and go back to the Cheyennes with a white scalp and the great horses. So when the woman went away, I went to the infant. It was not afraid, Thunder Moon. It lifted up its hands to me. I could not help picking it up and carrying it away with me. I said that the Sky People knew that I wanted fast horses, and a son, and they had led me where I could find both! So I carried the child away. I was hunted for many days by the white men. But at last I came to the open country, and then nothing could keep me from winning that race, for the chestnuts were working under me! That is the story, Thunder Moon. You know how you have grown up in my tepee. My blood is not your blood. My thoughts are not your thoughts. I am Suhtai, and you are not. But a place is in my heart for you; tell me if there is a place in yours for me?"

"Hear me, Sky People!" cried Thunder Moon enthusiastically. "I know that you brought me into the plains so that I could live with your chosen race. As for my real father and mother, they are nothing to me; I only know the lodge of Big Hard Face. Therefore I never—"

"Speak slowly!" said the wise old brave. "There is nothing so easily broken as a promise a man does not want to keep. If you have not seen your father and your mother, nevertheless, they have seen you. If you have forgotten them, they have not forgotten you!''

"What do you mean?" asked Thunder Moon, much disturbed.

"Tarawa has heed of the white man and the black, as well as of the red," declared the old chief. "So he has knowledge of you here, and of course he has had knowledge of the sorrow of your father and your mother!"

Thunder Moon fell into great trouble, but at last he said hurriedly, "I shall tell you. If they have not forgotten me, then they are dead. I do not feel them calling to my heart!"

"You will hear them afterward," said the chief. "Now you are too full of trouble because of the woman. Because of her, you will have more troubles still. Now let us go home, Thunder Moon. Still for a little time my lodge is your lodge, and my home is your home. Afterward, you will begin to turn to your own people. Ah, and I have been like a fool! If one clips the wing of an eagle, still the feathers will grow again!"

To this, Thunder Moon began an emotional protest that he never would leave the lodge of his foster father, and that to the end of his life he would be true to him and remain—

Big Hard Face cut him short, saying bluntly, "I am old, and old men love to talk much, but not to listen."

So they walked on in silence, and Big Hard Face went slower and slower, till it seemed as though he were changing his mind with every step that he made.

"Go slow, go slowly!" said the chief. "I am not a boy. I am not a young buck. I am very old!"

When they came to the edge of the camp, December declared that he wished to walk to see a friend, and he added bitterly to his foster son, "Besides, you will want to go off by yourself and think of this thing—and how you come from strange people—and how quickly you can go to see their faces! At least, you will want to run to see the woman!"

Big Hard Face walked off alone, and Thunder Moon went quietly back toward his tepee, his head raised so high that the lights of the stars twisted and swirled and dazzled in his eyes, and wild new thoughts and fears and hopes began to storm through his brain.

He would have walked, in this fashion, straight into the

hands of death but for the glint of the danger he saw with the corner of his eyes and leaped aside from. He whirled in time to meet the lunging shadow and the knife that was its darting point. He grappled with the brave who held the weapon, and then with an exclamation of horror he sprang back from the murderer; for he had recognized Snake-that-talks, one of his oldest and closest friends in the tribe.

CHAPTER

27

The other did not attempt to skulk away. For a moment he poised the knife flat in the palm of his hand, as though ready to hurl it at Thunder Moon; but then—perhaps realizing that this was a weak defense against the "medicine" that hung in the holster beside the other's thigh—he dropped the weapon back into its sheath and folded his arms. There was no finer presence among all the tall ranks of the Suhtai than Snake-that-talks, and in the starlight he made an imposing figure.

"Brother," said Thunder Moon sadly, "we have been friends for many years. With you I went on the war trail when we entered the land of the Comanches and took away their great medicine, the Yellow Man. Your lodge has been open to me, and my lodge has been open to you. In the winter famines we have given meat to one another. Of the last pemmican in your lodge, I have taken half. But now you have come to kill me! How have I wronged you, brother? What do I own that should be yours?"

The Suhtai seemed unable to answer for a moment, but

then he said slowly, "The woman in your tepee smiled at me. That is all!"

"It is Red Wind again!" groaned Thunder Moon. "She is not a woman but an evil spirit! Oh, Snake-that-talks, you already have a squaw and two children in your lodge!"

To this, the Indian made no answer, and Thunder Moon turned away and stumbled toward his home. For Red Wind, he kept a strange fury in his mind; for he knew that she had stolen away one of his nearest friends with a single glance. Why, though, had he spared the life of the young brave? For that very reason Snake-that-talks never would forgive him!

When Thunder Moon came closer to his tepee, he was aware of a number of young men loitering here and there and he passed slowly among them, expecting that they had been drawn there by a wish to speak with him—perhaps to propose some feat of war. However, not one of them paid any attention to him but allowed him to go past them, while they continued to stroll in an apparently aimless manner. But what could have brought them there? Thunder Moon could not guess, unless, indeed, it were the singing of a girl within the tepee of his foster father. A rich, low-pitched, rather husky voice was chanting a song that was strange to the ears of Thunder Moon, and he understood instantly why the loiterers were gathered in front of his lodge. It was Red Wind's song that had brought them, as surely as summer skies bring the birds. It was Red Wind's song, also, that made these youthful warriors oblivious to his coming. And all at once his passions mastered him and carried him away, like a boat sloping down a lee tide. For he felt that this girl who sat in his tepee was bringing about him vast dangers that, sooner or later, must overwhelm him.

So he strode into the entrance of the lodge.

The moment he appeared the song stopped, as though he had struck the singer; and yonder sat Red Wind, staring down at the ground in all humility.

Or was it humility, indeed? Suddenly he felt more hate than kindness for her—hatred and fear mixed together, for he wanted to catch her by the arm and drag her to a place where the firelight would shine upon her guilty face, but he dared not touch her.

"Red Wind!" he said.

She lifted her head obediently and looked toward him. But she might as well have continued to stare at the ground, so dense was the veil which she had dropped across her eyes.

"I have met Snake-that-talks!" said he, and waited to see the flickering shadow of guilt cross her face.

No shadow touched it. She was like one who sleeps with open eyes.

White Crow slipped nearer, her eyes hungry with mischief, as though she guessed that trouble was about to descend upon the head of the young woman, and as though she reveled in the prospect.

"Go out from the tepee!" Thunder Moon commanded her.

"It is come to this!" whined White Crow. "I am driven out from the lodge which I made with my own hands! Who else cleaned all those buffalo hides? Who prepared them? Who set up this tepee, so that it looked like a pyramid of snow in the spring? And now you are driving me away to shiver in the cold and—"

A wave of Thunder Moon's arm convinced her that she would have to obey, and she shuffled through the entrance and disappeared.

"Now," said Thunder Moon to the girl, "let me know what it is that you want!"

She looked up at him, her eyes still vague, though a meaning was beginning to come into them.

"Snake-that-talks is a great warrior," said Thunder Moon in continuation. "There is hardly a braver or a keener man among the Suhtai. You showed that you are clever and wise when you picked him out and sent him to murder me!"

She closed her eyes.

"Murder?" breathed the girl.

He strove fiercely to understand what was in her voice— horror, or disappointment, or perhaps merely fear of the punishment that now might hang over her head.

"You sent him," said the warrior. "You put the knife in

his hand and you sent him out to find me and to kill me. Then you would go to his lodge and be his squaw!''

With a curious detachment, she looked up to him as he stood in the firelight, a giant form, with his shadow floating on the white tepee wall behind him. Light-footed, massive of shoulder, proud of head, if ever man walked who seemed typical of all that an Indian warrior should be, such seemed the foster son of December on this very night when he had learned that he was not an Indian.

''Confess it!'' said he, grown more savage during her silence. For a strange fear was entering him. At one moment she seemed to him the only reality he ever had looked upon; and again she seemed a very maya of beautiful illusion. ''But you knew that he had tried and failed. Some shadowy owl or bat flew into your lodge and sat on your shoulder, so that the old eyes of White Crow could not see it. It told you everything that had happened.''

Such stories he had used for his mirth, in another day; but now he looked upon her seriously as an occultist, for how else to define her he knew not.

She said quietly, ''Do you believe in talking birds?''

''I believe in evil spirits, and I know that there is one in you,'' cried he. ''No other woman could do as you have done. There is nothing but danger and harm in you. To your father you showed that. Now you show it to me! And I cannot tell why I do not tie you hand and foot and set you out on the prairie where the wolves might eat you!''

She said, rather in curiosity than in fear, he thought, ''The promise you gave to my father keeps you from doing that.''

''When you put a knife in the hand of Snake-that-talks,'' replied Thunder Moon, ''you set me free from that oath.''

''Here is the only knife that I own,'' said she. ''Was it this knife that Snake-that-talks used against you?''

''You looked at him,'' replied Thunder Moon, ''and the evil spirit in you possessed him! Now you have called other young men of the Suhtai together. They stand in front of my lodge and listen to your voice and every one of them has a knife ready against me! Why do you do these things, Red Wind? How have I harmed you? When have I laid a heavy hand upon you? Have I forced you to become my squaw against your will? Have I beaten you to make you do more work? Have I forced you to carry heavy weights, or to flesh the hides, or to wear your eyes and your quick fingers putting beads upon moccasins? In what way have I wronged you or been cruel to you?"

The heart of the warrior swelled in him as he spoke. In all the epos of his life, nothing had stirred him so much as this interview with the maiden of the Omissis.

"You have not wronged me," said the girl. "It is my father who has wronged me."

He breathed more freely. But he added, "Then what can I do to make you happy? What can I do to keep you from arming my best friends against me?"

"When I first came to you," said the girl, in her quiet voice, "you could have taken the price of the fifty horses and given it back to my father, and given me back to him along with it."

"Do you wish me to do that?" he asked her.

"I wished it then," said she. "I think that I wished it then. But now it is too late. Now I think that it is much too late!"

"Why is it too late, Red Wind?"

"If you would think about it a little, quietly, then you would know why."

He grew wildly angry again. Once, as he rode the plains, he had seen a hawk strike a small bird in midair, and lighting on a stunted tree, hackle it with talons and beak. So he was moved to throw himself on this strange creature and destroy her because of the mystery she opposed against him at all times.

"Am I a child without wits?" he asked the girl. "Have I not thought about this thing until my brain aches?"

"Yes," she agreed, unheedful of his passion, "I suppose that thinking may not help, after all. Either one knows, or one does not know!"

"I shall do it!" exclaimed Thunder Moon. "I shall gather together all the treasure that your father gave to us. If it were ten times as great, it would not be great enough to make up for the pain I suffer in keeping you. I shall gather everything together, and more, and take you with the price back to the Omissis!''

"When will you do it?'' she asked.

"I? Tomorrow!''

She smiled, faintly.

"Why do you smile, Red Wind? You make me very angry when you act as though you knew things I cannot know.''

She wove her fingers into one massive braid of her hair and watched him.

"I think it is too late for me and for you,'' she said sadly. "I don't think that you will give back the price to my father or give me back with it. And there is nothing but trouble before us!''

He was about to speak again, when Big Hard Face entered the tepee and so the conversation was quickly broken off.

CHAPTER

28

White Crow entered almost behind her nephew. The ancient woman was trembling with malice.

"This wicked witch," she cried to December, "has been sitting here singing love songs and gathering the young men around the lodge!"

"Wait!" broke in Thunder Moon. "They were not love songs. I heard her singing."

"Whatever she sings is a love song!" exclaimed White Crow. "The young men came and walked before the tepee. Then you drove me out, as if I were a dog! And the young men came to me one by one. 'Is all well with Red Wind?' they asked. They could hear you talking loudly to her, and they frowned when they heard the loudness of your voice! Do you see what the curse is that she has brought to this lodge, Big Hard Face?"

That chief, however, had retired to the darkness that surrounded his couch and there he sat, almost lost to view. White Crow peered at him, opened her withered lips to say something more, and then peered more closely and discovered that even the dimness of that place was not sufficiently dark for Big Hard Face. He had covered his head with his robe, like one who mourns.

At that, her malice seemed to grow in her. She hurried closer. In her dangling arms there seemed as much lean, sinewy strength as ever; but her back was bent with years.

"Son," she said to the old chief, "what is the sorrow that has fallen on you?"

He did not answer.

And then she screamed at him, shaking her bony fists, "I am not a woman! I am dirt! I am nothing! I only live to work till I die. No one will listen to me. No heart is open to me. In my own lodge, that I made with my own hands, I am nothing! But I shall not endure it! The river will take my body. Or I can go to the lodge of a friend—"

"Be quiet!" said Thunder Moon, angrily. "All the ears in every tepee near us will hear you!"

"Let them hear me!" shrieked the squaw. "I shall go now and sing my song in front of the lodge and let them know how I live here!"

The deep, lifeless voice of the chief spoke to her. "Woman, woman, make no more noise. Or else, sit in the ashes and weep, but not for yourself."

At this solemn speech, White Crow clung to the post from which the medicine bag and the weapons of Big Hard Face hung.

"What has happened?" she whispered.

"We are alone," said December.

"We are not alone," said the squaw, mistaking his meaning. "The evil woman from the Omissis is here with us, and Thunder Moon, who thinks I am only a dog!"

"We are alone," said the chief, more solemnly than before. "Thunder Moon is gone. He is drawn away to his own people!"

"What are his people?" gasped the squaw. "Are they not our people? Are not you his father? Does he not belong to the Suhtai, sing their songs, fight their battles? Big Hard Face, do not talk like a fool!"

"He is gone to his own people," answered the chief again.

"The Omissis girl opened his eyes: She showed him the truth. Soon we shall lose him. Now, let me be in peace!"

And he drew the robe slowly over his head again.

White Crow, as though suddenly gone blind, reached about until she found Thunder Moon, and then she clung to him. All the days of his life, he had received little but hard words and sharp actions from her, but now she burst into a terrible complaint, not in a screaming voice such as she had used before, but in a shuddering whisper, still holding close to him, clutching at his hands, or reaching up to stroke his head with her fingers, hard as bone.

"Child, child!" said White Crow. "Big Hard Face is dying of grief. Besides what he has told you is not true. He is your father. He prayed to the Sky People for you. They heard him. They called him a great distance. They placed you before him. He took you and came back to his people. You are their gift to us. He has no child; I have no boy and no girl; and if you go we are like burned grass. We are like grass that has been burned by the roots. The wind blows us away from the earth. The moment you leave us, we begin to wait for our death. When you leave us, you kill us. Thunder Moon, have pity on me! Have pity on that old man!"

She fell upon her knees, clasping his hands.

"It is because I have said bitter words to you, like the old, wicked fool that I am!" moaned White Crow. "But I have been evil in speech because I was zealous to make you the greatest warrior in the nation. I wanted to see you fly above the heads of other men, like an eagle. I always have loved you, and now—"

Thunder Moon leaned and raised the withered body in his mighty arms.

"Do you think that I shall go?" said he. "No, now I swear to you that—"

"Thunder Moon!" said the clear, sudden voice of the girl. "Ask your heart if you should swear! You have a real mother!"

And the words were stopped on his lips, for into his heart was thrust a strange, new hunger that had been growing up there ever since the story of his foster father had been told to him earlier in the evening. He could tell himself that he was a Cheyenne and that he detested the whites and all their ways. And he even could tell himself that he loved his foster father, and even that he was fond of the squaw, White Crow. But, at the same time, it was necessary for him to admit that he turned with all his soul toward the unknown man and the unknown woman who were his real parents. So the oath he was about to take stopped in his throat.

White Crow with a strangled cry of rage, rushed at the Omissis girl. Over her she stood, her fists clenched, and poured out denunciation in a screaming voice.

"You have stolen him!" wailed White Crow. "Why do you want him? It is not for yourself. It is only to torment us. It is only to break the heart of December. There is no woman in the world so wicked as you are. You were a whip and a wound to your father. You were like a winter wolf, eating your own kind. Now you come to eat us! But I shall stop you! You will do no more harm to us or to others!"

So she said, and clutched the great war club that leaned against the post at the foot of the couch of the chief. Before Thunder Moon could stop her, she swayed the weapon over her head, and Red Wind, like one recognizing doom, made no motion to avoid the stroke but waited with calm upward-gazing eyes. It was Big Hard Face himself who swept like a shadow from his place and took White Crow, weapon and all, in his arms. Still she struggled. But she had begun to sob. Weeping overcame her, and she lay in the darkness, moaning, and beating her hands against her breast, while Big Hard Face sat beside her, speaking like a mother to a child.

Thunder Moon stepped from the lodge as from a place of pestilence. The young men had vanished: All the camp was still. But in the neighboring tepees, he knew that many an ear was listening to the groans of the old squaw, and that the same ears had listened also, to the preceding altercations.

A soft step behind him, and he turned and looked down into the face of Red Wind. She bowed her head upon the tethering post that stood before the tent and leaned heavily against it.

"Are you not happy?" asked Thunder Moon, standing

above her and towering in wrath. "You have left everyone in the lodge of my father sick at heart. It is your work. When have you had a better day? Since the sun set on this day, you have stepped between me and Standing Antelope; you have broken the heart of my father; you have crushed White Crow, and you have torn me from my people. You have made me a man without a nation. I have no people; I have no home; I am no more than a dead leaf blowing over the prairie; I am more friendless than an old buffalo bull, cast out by the herd! Tell me, Red Wind! Is not this a perfect day for you?"

She did not raise her head, and her voice was a little muffled as she answered, "Will you go, then, quickly? Will you go at once back to your own people?"

He was startled by this implied admission of all evil in her answer.

"After a little while," said Thunder Moon, "everything is understood even about the buzzard and the crow. They keep their lives because other things on the prairies die. So I know about you. You cannot be happy until you have driven me away from my people! But still you do not tell me why you hate me!"

"Listen to me!" said the girl, straightening and turning to face him. "Already you have many enemies among the Suhtai. You are not a chief. You never will be a chief. And yet all the young chiefs are afraid of you and therefore they hate you! Snake-that-talks has tried to murder you. He is a great young chief. Others are like him. They have pretended to love you, but they hate you. You have taken the son of Three Bears away and brought him back a warrior with a name. Do you think that Three Bears loves you because of that? No, he would bury his bullet in your heart if he dared! So it is with the others. You are white! You are white! You are white! Go back to the white men. You are not wanted here!"

Wounded vanity did not master Thunder Moon then because so many blows had fallen upon him recently that he was untouched except by the greatest things.

"There is only one thing that would keep me here, I think," he answered her at last. "That is to learn why you hate me, Red Wind!"

"Ask a woman why she hates and ask the wind why it blows!" said the girl savagely. "All that I know is that I hate you. I do not want to be near you. Stand far from me, Thunder Moon!"

He hesitated over her, his breath coming in jerks.

"Do you wish to stab me when I touch you?" he asked.

"Once I have proved it to you," said she.

"Yes, yes," he nodded. And he stretched out his hand and took in it the heavy, silken braid of her hair. And it gave him strange pleasure and strange pain to see her wince from his touch.

"I have thought a little bit about women," said he, "but they have been good women that I thought I would take into my tepee one day. However, I cannot tell. It may be that this is the best. I have loved fighting and the war trail. But what is that danger compared to the danger of you, Red Wind? Ha! I know why your father gave you that name! It is because you are like a mist of blood blowing; you are like a cloud of fire sweeping through the sky; you are peril worse than poisoned air. Perhaps it would be a great pleasure to be loved by you. Perhaps it is a greater pleasure to be hated by you. See, Red Wind, how much you are pleased to torture me. My life was a big life. When men looked at the Suhtai they saw Thunder Moon first. The rest lived in his shadow. Now, I am nothing. But perhaps I am pleased to torture you, in turn. I touch you, and your soul is sick. I think that I shall stay here and sleep among the Suhtai tonight, and all the nights to come. And every night I shall not dare to close my eyes more than a wolf, for fear of your knife and the knives of your lovers. But night and day I shall watch you to see that you take your poison into the life of no other man! I have spoken; so let it be between us!"

She, listening to him, seemed eager once or twice to speak, but before he ended, horror seemed to master her, and she began to shrink backward toward the entrance to the lodge. So, as he ended, she stepped past his view and disappeared into the interior of the tepee.

Still, from inside, came the weary, endless sobbing of White Crow. It was impossible for Thunder Moon to enter the lodge upon this night. He went from the village and sat on the top of a hummock under the open heavens where he could have clear view of the stars, which are the faces of the Sky People. He felt that this day had divorced him from everything that was old and tried and proved of worth in his life, and so he was pressed up closer to those invisible patrons who had sheltered him. The night grew old, and the high wail of a coyote on the horizon told of the coming of day, and all the stars on the field of night began to wither and turn pale and small, but still he did not move from his place.

CHAPTER

29

Man had failed Thunder Moon, and now the wide book of the sky, where always before he had been able to read some sign, offered him a blank. He rose from his watching with the feeling that he had come to the end of an old trail.

In the cold, early dawn he came shivering back into the village. Even the dogs had not gained their morning vigor, and snarled at one another half-heartedly, their tails tucked between their legs; but the warriors were astir. Nearly a hundred braves had been assembled and were preparing to leave the village.

On what errand?

And then the heart of Thunder Moon swelled with anxiety and anger as he noted the war paint on their faces and all the familiar preparations that were made only for a warpath excursion of the first importance. In all the recent years, not one such expedition had left the camp except that which had ridden to disaster against Falling Stone and his victorious Pawnees. With his single hand he had demonstrated that the medicine of Spotted Bull, who had excluded him from that trail, had been false medicine. But now another and a most important work was at hand and of it he had not been even apprised!

He gathered himself in his robe and stalked slowly through the mustering ranks of the warriors, and with the utmost diligence they avoided his eye, busying themselves with their accoutrements and speaking eagerly to one another.

But he could feel the glances of those who were in his rear turn after him, and he could hear their soft whispers; also, he felt the vibration of stifled laughter. They were mocking him behind his back. How long would it be, then, before they mocked him to his face?

He remembered what the girl had said. They did not love him, these Suhtai, no matter how many victories he had given to them. And he could understand that that was the case. He was not one of them.

He passed Snake-that-talks. Time had been when this doughty warrior would not so much as try to catch a prairie dog without first appealing for the advice of Thunder Moon. Now the brave regarded him with a sullen face that gave him no greeting whatever.

He passed Standing Antelope. And the boy flushed with shame, but turned his head hastily away so that he might not see the older warrior.

At that, the heart of Thunder Moon leaped in him. He drew his robe closer about him, and so came to the lodge of Spotted Bull from which the last of the selected warriors were issuing. The medicine man turned upon Thunder Moon with a broad leer of malice and triumph.

Once again Spotted Bull had made medicine that proclaimed that no fortune would accompany any expedition in which Thunder Moon rode; once again he had been believed; and once more the insult was cast upon the shoulders of the warrior.

He endured it as well as he could; but he walked on slowly, dying with an agony of injured pride and sorrow and despair. Yet he could see the reason for it all. In his own mind the history of past events he had heard or witnessed remained as important as the tall forms of hills, ever present. But to the

Suhtai and to all other Indians the past was a pleasant or a terrible legend; the future was a misty dream; and only the present was of importance. What did it matter that Spotted Bull had been proved a lying impostor one day, if, on the next, he seemed to dispel a thunderstorm? And so on the present occasion, he was believed implicitly when he prophesied that no good fortune could come to the warriors if they allowed Thunder Moon to ride out in their midst.

He went gloomily on through the village until he came to the lodge of his foster father. Big Hard Face sat in the tepee, with Red Wind nearby, working or pretending to work at the beading of a pair of moccasins. White Crow was not present, and the warrior was glad of her absence.

He said briefly, "It is time for me to go to see the face of my mother. Will you tell me how the trail runs?"

Red Wind did not look up, but her fingers froze at their work. However, the chief, without alteration of countenance, leaned forward and began to trace his sketch for the journey on the ground.

For a quarter of a century he had not ridden over that ground, but now he was able to draw the plan accurately, presenting many details. He talked in terms of days' marches, and he indicated the main features that would be encountered, or else he sketched the chief landmarks by which the direction would be taken.

Another Suhtai would have carried all these instructions in his mind. But Thunder Moon had no such gifts of visual memory. On a thin strip of antelope hide he reproduced the sketch as it was made to grow on the ground; and then, rolling up the strip, he knew that he had his book of directions ready at hand in case of leaving the trail.

After that, he got his favorite dream shield, his war spear, his best rifle, and two revolvers. The weight of this equipment seemed out of proportion to the amount of food that he carried. But he must live by his weapons when he was on the road. Shooting is never so accurate as when the day's pot depends upon it. So Thunder Moon was equipped for a great journey. Now he tried the edge of his hunting knife and adjusted his medicine bag, which was a little squirrel skin containing a few small pebbles. He had no belief in medicine bags. His wearing of this one was simply a concession to the social will of the tribe. A man without a medicine bag was as inconceivable as a man without a head, well nigh. This bag he donned last of all of his equipment.

When it was secured about his neck; hanging by a thin rope of braided horsehair, he said to his foster father, "This is a long trail. But I had better start on it at once. The young men of the Suhtai do not love me. I hope in Tarawa that they will not be crushed while I am away. But if they ever should come to me to be helped, tell them that Thunder Moon is thinking about them, and that some of their faces and some of their words he cannot forget. They are marked down in his heart; perhaps one day he will be written down in theirs! But now I start on a long trail where only one other Cheyenne has ridden before me. And I know that I may leave my scalp on the way and my spirit may go on before me. Therefore, my father, let all things be clear between us. If you have given me a home and a name among the Suhtai, let it be said that I have given you love and obedience. If you have given me food and shelter for a long time, now I give to you everything that I have won by my hands, except Sailing Hawk, the weapons that I hold now, my saddle, and the meat that I carry with me. But the beaded suits, and the rifles, and the painted robes, and the beads and the knives and the clubs and the captured medicine bags of our enemies, and everything else that I have—even to the eagle feathers that are used for the headdress of chiefs and to ornament our shields—I give to you."

Still Red Wind sat with her head bowed, and her hands frozen at their work. But the chief answered slowly, "This is such a gift as a man makes when he is about to die. Do you go out with no hope, Thunder Moon?"

"No," said the warrior, "but I go with the knowledge that I must leave my old life behind me. That is well. I am not sorry. Someday I shall come back to you, and then I shall be all Indian or all white man! Now I am only a mongrel, neither wolf nor dog. The dogs snarl at me, and the wolves have their teeth bared against me!"

"Farewell!" said the old man, raising his hand.

From his pipe he blew a puff to the ground and another he wafted toward the sky. He handed the pipe to Thunder Moon, who imitated the example.

"Farewell!" said Thunder Moon.

He turned sharply on Red Wind.

"You have done much harm in this tepee," said he. "Also, there still may be much harm left in you. There may be good, also. You have driven me away. Stay here and help White Crow. She is old and your hands are young and strong. As for me, I forgive you."

She would not look up to him, nor answer a word, and he was rather surprised that her malice was so complete. He hurried from the lodge, a great lump in his throat; but just beyond the threshold he hesitated for a moment, for it seemed to him that he heard the stifled sobbing of a woman from inside the tepee. He told himself that it could be no more than the crying of a child in a neighboring lodge. So he mounted the stallion and took his way through the camp.

CHAPTER

30

He lingered for no other farewells, but heading straight across the open prairies toward the east and south, he settled the tall stallion to a raking trot that shuffled the miles rapidly behind him. North and west, in just the opposite direction from that which he had taken, he could see the dwindling cloud of dust that told of the war party advancing slowly toward the realm of the hardy Pawnees; and again his heart swelled with indignation. Twice, as though in answer to his returning thought, Sailing Hawk slackened to a walk, tossing his head, and twice with a renewed resolution, the warrior sent the stallion on again.

Thunder Moon had squared his shoulders against the back trail for some time when a regular pulse of sound behind him made him glance backward, and he saw a rider coming at full gallop.

A dim, dark hope rose in his mind that some enemy of his within the village, feeling that the medicine of Thunder Moon must have become very weak, had started on his trail to avenge some old disgrace. But as the rider came closer he made out in amazement the slender form of young Standing Antelope.

The latter, approaching swiftly, raised his right hand in greeting; and as he came closer, he asked by signs if he could open a parley with his big friend. So Thunder Moon waved him in and Standing Antelope came to a halt beside him.

"The braves listen to the voice of Spotted Bull," said the boy simply. "I have listened, too, and for a moment I forgot that Thunder Moon had given me my name, let me count my first coup, and call myself a man. I have given up the war party. I came back to ask you to forgive me; I found that you were gone; I was afraid that I never should find you again."

"How did you pick up my trail?" asked Thunder Moon curiously.

"What other horse steps as far as Sailing Hawk?" asked the boy. "Besides, he is not a bird; he makes a mark when he steps!" He pointed to the big, black round hoofs of the tall horse, and Thunder Moon smiled a little. It eased his heart to see the keen eyes of this lad, and to know that in this case, at least, a lost friend had returned to him.

But he said, "I am going on a trail that may fill twelve moons; and I never may return."

"If I live to be a very old man," replied Standing Antelope, "I never can die better than by the side of Thunder Moon. If we are away for one snow, or for two, it is better. I may come back a man!"

"Turn back when you will," said Thunder Moon. "The trail will be long, and if your heart becomes empty and many marches are between us and the Suhtai, go when you wish." The boy smiled at this suggestion that he might weary of the work, and drawing back two lengths and a little to the windward of his leader to escape the dust, he followed obediently in the trail his master had laid out.

Travel in the prairies is like travel over the ocean, with an unbroken horizon and no steady drift of landmarks past the eyes. By midafternoon the sun was sharp and hot; and they had put many an hour of long, weary travel behind them; and then for all their labor they had no real sense of distance covered. All before them was as it had been when they left the Cheyenne village.

Now, however, a thin cloud of dust before them began to grow in size and distinctness. Standing Antelope volunteered to scout ahead. He came back in an hour to report that he had made out a long caravan stretched across the prairie—a long host of wagons and riders one behind the other, with outlying groups of guards or hunters riding over the plains.

"If I am a white man," said Thunder Moon to his heart, "why should I not join these people and journey along with them?" He added aloud, "Let us ride in and talk with them, Standing Antelope!"

"Ah, my father," said the youth, "do you smile when you say this? Do not the Suhtai say that it is safer to trust the Pawnees than the whites?"

However, Thunder Moon insisted, and the boy, sitting stiff in his saddle, most uneasy, followed his leader, his hand constantly upon his rifle.

Three hunters, returning toward the caravan with their horses loaded with antelope meat, now swept in the direction of Thunder Moon and came up close to him. They were dressed in every respect like Indians, from buckskin, beaded shirts, to ornamented moccasins. The sun had darkened their skin, but the long hair that fell over their shoulders was not confined by a headband, and it was blond and faded by the weather. With their fierce, keen eyes, they estimated the value of the horse and the accoutrements of Thunder Moon. Every appointment was worthy of a chief and a great one, and the oldest of the three said in fairly good Cheyenne, "Suhtais, why are you here? Have you come to spy on us?"

That blunt question made the color fly into the face of Thunder Moon, but he said quietly, "There is much hunting to be done for such a tribe as yours. Let me travel with you and hunt. You shall pay me as you please for the meat that I bring in with my friend."

They looked at one another, murmured a few words, and then the oldest answered, "Come in with us. We'll take you to the chief of the caravan."

They rode on in the lead, while Standing Antelope followed at the side of his master.

He said with deft, swift fingers in the sign language, "These three men want our rifles, and probably they want our scalps; and most of all they want Sailing Hawk. Even when they spoke to you, they insulted you with their first words and asked if you were a spy. Do not trust them, my father! Three shots and they are dead; we count three coups; and we carry their scalps and their horses and their rifles away with us!"

"Their backs are turned," said Thunder Moon.

"They are taking you into a trap."

"Turn back if you wish," answered the fingers of the warrior. "I am going in with them."

This challenge silenced the boy, but he was terribly ill at ease as they drew closer to the caravan. Now they could look through the dust mist that boiled up behind the first wagon and settled in white sheets, streaked with sweat, on the animals that plodded in the rear, and on the other wagons, and on the men who rode or walked near the procession. Returning from the distant plains where they had been trading with the Indians, this caravan was chiefly loaded with buffalo hides. For weeks they had been on the way; and for more weeks they would continue traveling. Considering the vast distances covered, the time spent, a white man would have wondered what profit could be in such trade. No such thought came to Thunder Moon. These toiling wagons, these unkempt men—ragged as wild Indians, and without their grace—were to him symbols of the white race, of toil, of slavery. Presently they came beside the rearmost wagon. There, striding beside a team of mules, was a monster of a man who turned aside at the hail of the three returning hunters and listened to what they had to say. All the while, he kept his bold, pale eyes fixed on the face of Thunder Moon, and at last he stepped forward and extended his hand. Thunder Moon took it, and instantly his fingers were almost crushed in a terrible grip. Almost crushed, but not quite; and, regaining a slight purchase, by a desperate effort Thunder Moon held his own, then made his hand break into the powerful pressure the white man exerted. He felt a tremor in the arm of the other; he saw amazement in the face of the stranger. Then his hand was suddenly set free.

"We can use you with our hunters," said the white leader of the caravan, using a blundering Cheyenne dialect. "But why are you here, my friend? Did you put a bullet into one of your own chiefs?"

He waited for no answer but strode away after his mule team. The three hunters, in the meantime, had found something in this interview that left them agape. Perhaps they were accustomed to seeing men crumple under the famous grip of the wagon boss. At any rate, they stared helplessly at Thunder Moon and at the faint smile he had maintained throughout this brief and silent test of his manhood. Then, suddenly, they began to smile at one another. Thunder Moon needed no knowledge of English to understand that he had been accepted in their society; and the first strain of apprehension was ended.

But what a society it was!

During the day, he saw little enough of the teamsters and traders, for he was away across the prairies with the boy, hunting. And only twice did they fail to find game. The instinct of Standing Antelope was marvelously sure; and the gun of Thunder Moon was no less unerring when the game was in sight. But at night they sat at a camp fire and watched scenes how different from those in an Indian camp! The merry laughter and the childish free-heartedness of the Cheyennes were here replaced by sullen, grumbling voices in a constant tone of complaint. And after the supper was eaten, cards or dice appeared and games were played in silence, broken only by a snarl. An infinite danger was in those threatening voices. On the evening of the third day after the Indians had joined this company they saw a revolver leap from a holster, saw the flash of the gun, and saw another man pitch on his face, dead.

Standing Antelope went aside with his leader, shuddering.

"These people are like bad spirits," said he. "If they kill each other, soon they will kill us! See! There is no blood kin of the dead man to kill his murderer. No one cares. No one is excited."

"See," said Thunder Moon, "they are gathering together. They have taken the weapons away from the killer. I think that something is going to happen."

"Perhaps they are taking those weapons as a price for the dead man's life."

"Perhaps. Let us watch, Standing Antelope. These are strange people. Who can tell what they will do? Who can understand them?"

"There is the chief coming."

Loughran, the giant who had matched grips with Thunder Moon, came into the circle. Quickly he selected twelve men. He talked to them a moment. The twelve raised their hands with a solemn demeanor and made some answer. After that, half a dozen men came forward. They pointed to the slayer, but they were addressing the twelve. The whole period of the deliberations did not occupy more than half an hour. Then the hands of the prisoner were tied behind him and he was led a little distance out into the plains where a wagon tongue was fixed in the ground, with a rope passed through its upper end. The noose settled around the throat of the destroyer. In another moment he was suspended in midair, kicking, violently.

"Let him down!" gasped Standing Antelope. "They have punished him enough!"

"They are going to let him die!" murmured Thunder Moon, a sweat standing on his brow.

"But then his spirit cannot get out of his mouth. It will die in his body and rot with his body if he is choked."

"That is true," said Thunder Moon. "Look! He struggles no more! He is dead!"

"But were all the others blood relations of the dead man?"

"I shall ask."

He stopped a passing wagoner and put the question. The latter said in answer, "That is law, Cheyenne. No murderer has a friend in our country. And we're all blood relations of the murdered man!"

"Law?" murmured Thunder Moon, as they watched the body of the murderer cut down and buried with some care. "What is law, Standing Antelope?"

"Death of the body and the spirit; death by hanging!" said

the boy. "I am very sick, Thunder Moon. Come away with me. I am afraid. These men are more brutal than beasts!"

"They are," said Thunder Moon. "But I think that there will be no more murders in this camp!"

Afterward, they went close to the spot where the dead man had been buried. They struck a light and found that a board had been put in the ground, and upon the board letters were carved with a knife.

"What does it mean?" asked the boy.

"It is medicine," said Thunder Moon. "This is a great medicine. What it means I cannot understand. But I shall never stop studying until I learn. Did you hear him? All are blood relations of a murdered man. That is law! Law, Standing Antelope, must be a very great mystery. It is one of their gods."

"The black robes do not talk about it," observed the boy.

"We know nothing about these people," said Thunder Moon. "Let us watch closely; there is a great deal to learn!"

CHAPTER

31

As the slow weeks of that journey went by, Thunder Moon began to learn the language of the whites by leaps and bounds. In the evening, he picked up a new store of words; all the next day as he voyaged over the plains with Standing Antelope, he rehearsed what he had heard; and when he returned in the evening, he attempted to use his stock. So his knowledge grew like a tropical plant, nursed by the heat of his great desire to know.

In the meantime, he was learning far more than words, as a matter of course. Some ten days after he joined the train, he was wakened by a stealthy movement near him, and felt his rifle being withdrawn from beneath his pillow. He grappled with a shadowy form, which crumpled under his grasp. And when a lantern was brought, it was found to be a brute-faced teamster. Loughran, captain of the train, offered Thunder Moon his choice of two remedies. The first was that he, Loughran, would have the fellow stripped to the waist and flogged. The second choice would place the matter in the hands of Thunder Moon himself. Thunder Moon, seeing that the other was of a respectable bulk, accepted the second alternative. He was very angry. Moreover, he felt that these white men must be convinced, sooner or later that he was a fighting man worthy of some respect. There was much amusement. By lantern light the crowd made a circle. Into it stepped the combatants, and Thunder Moon glided close and smote the blow that was to begin and end the battle. He merely struck the air and received a hard fist in return cunningly placed near the point of his chin, so that it felt as though a hammer had struck him in the back of the head.

For ten minutes Thunder Moon charged furiously at this elusive figure, while the spectators yelled with delight. But the brute-faced fellow seemed shod with wings; there was lead in each of his hands; and he struck when and where it pleased him. One of Thunder Moon's eyes puffed and closed. His cheek was gashed. His jaw was lined with purple bruises. And then he had his fury well cuffed out of him and began to take time for thought. It was not through superior strength or courage that he was being beaten. It was by the medicine of the white man—it was by the mysterious use of mind. He took notice, now, that the first blow that the other threatened to strike never landed; and that the second one was what usually went home. So he varied his own tactics. He let the feint of a left at the head go; then he stepped in, stopped, and smote the body of his foe. Fair and square his fist landed. Bones crunched under the impact. A dreadful cry burst and broke in the air. And the thief lay writhing on the ground.

Loughran tapped Thunder Moon on the shoulder.

"How did you learn that trick? He was a pug, Cheyenne!"

Which Thunder Moon did not understand, but what he *did* appreciate was that this battle gained him a new position in the camp. Thereafter, all men treated him with a consummate respect. And certainly no more attempts were made to steal from him during the night. As for the pugilist, he was placed in a wagon, a very sick man, and transported groaning to the end of the journey.

There was no vital danger to the caravan except in one instance, and that was well nigh both the first and the last. A sudden report came that Indians were sweeping toward them.

And then out of a draw the charging warriors were seen to come, while the caravan hastily tried to double itself into a circle, the head drawing back toward the tail, and the tail rushing forward to join the head. Once formed into a circle of wagons, the caravan would take a lot of beating. But if the Indians could insert the point of their wedge before the circle was joined, they could then open out the whole length of the caravan and slay as they pleased, as though a wild cat should sink its talons into the belly of a hedgehog before the little animal could roll into a ball. With wild shouting the wagons worked to make the circle, but they still lacked something of coming together when the first half a dozen of the Indians on racing horses neared the gap. And there was no defense from within except from Thunder Moon. Chance had placed him at the vital spot, and he did not think twice. Perhaps life seemed to him such a confused thing that he cared little whether he lived or died. At any rate, right through the closing gap in the wagons, with faithful young Standing Antelope scurrying behind him, he charged out at the enemy, shouting his war cry, a revolver in each hand. They were Pawnees, chosen warriors. And yet to his amazement they did not wait for his charge. One among them shouted loud commands. The others split away to left and right and scurried back to join the charging mass of their companions. And the next moment the circle joined—the wagon fort was complete! The Pawnees, not caring to try its strength surged back to a safe distance and sat down like wolves to watch while a single chief came forward, calling in Cheyenne for Thunder Moon. The latter advanced, gun in hand, and saw before him none other than that tried and famous enemy of the Suhtai, Falling Stone. The Pawnee leaped from his horse, threw down his weapons, and hurried forward on foot. His eye was gleaming not with hostility but with pleasure.

"Friend," said he, "my brother still lives and grows strong in his lodge, and every day he tells the Pawnees of the greatness of Thunder Moon. I have heard his story. If there is war between the Suhtai and the Pawnees, there is no war between Falling Stone and you. As for the white men, we should have split in between their wagons and eaten them as hawks eat mice. Now take a rich present from me. Take my rifle and my horse as a gift. Go off in peace with honor to the Suhtai. And leave me here to deal with these white men!''

"Falling Stone is a great chief," answered Thunder Moon. "But now I ride with these white men. They are my friends. If you fight with them, you fight with me. But be wise, Falling Stone. There are many guns in that circle of wagons. And the men shoot straighter than Pawnees or Cheyennes. You will lose many of your braves and gain nothing.''

The Pawnee frowned and looked eagerly along the wagons, over which the dust cloud was beginning to blow away. Everywhere was the glint of rifles prepared for the battle. Then he nodded.

"I have lost a great prize for your sake," said he. "But I would lose one still greater and yet be able to smile. But my gun and my horse are yours; remember me for their sake.''

"Here," said Thunder Moon, "is a belt of beads for which I gave five strong horses. Take it, and remember me when you strap it on. And if on another day we meet in battle, let us yet see one another. There are other enemies for each of us.''

So they parted, Falling Stone walking off happily with the belt, and Thunder Moon taking his own prizes back to the wagons. He was received there like a hero. Whatever suspicion and dislike had surrounded him before, now vanished; and a crowd gathered to thank him for what he had done. There were more than thanks, however. When camp was made for that night, Loughran brought to him a good horse whose pack saddle was loaded down with all that an Indian could value. Guns, ammunition, knives, beadwork, sugar, coffee composed that load. And every wagon in the circle had made a contribution to the burden.

"Look!" said Thunder Moon to Standing Antelope. "They are good people, after all. They are not what they seemed at first!''

"You saved them the price of a thousand horses," replied the boy. "They have given you the price of five. That is good business for them.''

For the young Suhtai remained irreconcilable to the end.

That end came not many days later when, as they camped at night, they saw far before them the glimmering lights of the town that was the end of the wagon trip. Half the teamsters and hunters had scoured away to get to the waiting saloons in the town, and Thunder Moon and Standing Antelope went with them. Cautiously they moved through the crowds. But they were not noticed. Other Indians stalked through the mob, unheeded. Everywhere was a confused turmoil of many tongues accented by occasional salvos of pistol shots.

So after they had walked up and down through the noisy streets, Thunder Moon and the boy withdrew to the edge of the plains and the silence of the night.

"Now tell me about these people with white skins," said he to Standing Antelope.

"No man can understand them," replied the boy. "Because they have many minds in each head. One day they are great traders; the next day they are foolish hunters; one day they are wise in council; the next day they chatter like foolish crows; one day they are rich with beads and robes; the next night they have given all that they possess for the sake of fire water, which they put into their bellies, and it makes them sick. They are partly wise and they are partly mad. Let us leave these people, Thunder Moon. We have each of us only one mind. Let us go back to the Suhtai where it is easier to know men!"

"Let us sleep," said Thunder Moon sadly. "In the morning we shall talk again."

CHAPTER

32

Morning came, the first gray touch of light, and Thunder Moon, rising, saw that Standing Antelope was already up and had his horse saddled.

"Which way?" said the boy.

"Here is a horse packed heavily with rich things," said the warrior. "Take it and go back to the Suhtai. Here is enough to make you a wealthy man. You may have your own lodge and take wives. But I must go on. It is not what I want to do. But it is where I must go! The trail is not ended for me."

"Go on then," said the youth. "I cannot help following. But now I know that I never shall see my father's face again—and Three Bears has only one son!"

However, he could not be persuaded to depart, and straightway Thunder Moon turned more sharply to the south and east. And day by day they journeyed, now across open country; now they skirted the edges of the settlements of the whites, far advanced from the places where Big Hard Face had found them twenty years before. The landmarks that that hero had noted down were gone, almost without exception.

Forests had been leveled. New ones had been planted and were half grown. Even Standing Antelope, to whom the story of the trail had been disclosed, was at a loss.

The time came, however, they had to leave the plains definitely behind them and plunge straight in through the lands of the whites.

They traveled entirely by night, sleeping through the day in the shelter of some copse or heavy forest. Now they crossed a region chiefly given over to the grazing of cattle, with great distances between the houses. Leaving that region behind them, they came to a district where the vegetation was richer. There was still a good deal of forest, and there was a good deal of marshland; but all else was closely cultivated soil, the fields were smaller and smaller, and each was hedged with walls of stone, or with rail fences. They would have had most difficult going here, on account of the marshes and the many small streams, had it not been for the miracles of which Big Hard Face had told long before—and hardly been believed when he described them. These were the roads that pushed straight ahead, regardless of obstacles, cutting through high, built up over low, and advancing through the marshes by causeways and over the rivers by means of great bridges.

Now and then, too, they saw the sparkling lights of a great town in the distance; and once they lodged all day in a wood with the many noises of a large village murmuring or crashing about their ears so that they could not sleep. It was easy to find food. With every house went a poultry yard, and in every poultry yard they could help themselves. If a noisy dog disturbed them at their work of foraging, the active knife of Standing Antelope quickly silenced the disturber.

So they went on, day by day, striking deeper and deeper into a strange country.

"If all the Sioux, all the Blackfeet, all the Comanches, all the Pawnees, and all the Cheyennes were gathered together and brought here, could they fill so many villages as we have seen?" asked Thunder Moon. And the boy shook his head.

"And still we are not at the end of the white man's country. How, Standing Antelope, can we beat these people in any great war?"

"By the help of Tarawa, who gave us the plains," said the boy confidently. "And just as easily as we wring the throats of the fowls, so we could steal in and cut the throats of the sleepers in those lodges!"

Thunder Moon said nothing in reply, but he was beginning to have many doubts. All that Red Wind had said had come true.

But now they drew closer to their goal. All else on the landscape had been greatly changed, but the streams Big Hard Face had crossed still flowed in the same places, and by that network of water, Standing Antelope recovered the old trail.

And so, by the march of half a night they came at length about the middle hour of darkness to a great stretch of land where all the houses were gathered as Big Hard Face had said, in the lee of a mighty mansion filled with lights. And when they came still closer, they could examine the prodigious size of the house.

From its open doors and windows—for the night was warm—music floated, a girl singing, and the tinkling of some instrument that kept both the time and the key of her song with marvelous precision and beauty.

Thunder Moon listened, amazed.

"Why do you tremble, Standing Antelope?" he whispered.

"Because it is not like anything that I have dreamed," said the boy. "I am afraid because it is unknown! Is it not a spirit that makes the music, my father?"

"We shall go to see!"

"Let me stay here. My heart is very weak."

"Stay here, then. I shall come again before long!"

He started away, and Standing Antelope trembled again in the darkness.

Presently he heard a loud barking, and a furious snarling from some dog apparently of the largest size. That clamor ended abruptly, and the boy, with a faint smile, touched the handle of his knife. He, also, understood how to silence such a noisemaker. After that, he waited for a long, long time. The music ended, began again, ended and began again. A man was singing with a girl.

Finally Standing Antelope could stand it no longer, but went forward to find his companion. Across the open lawn he went, and through two hedges, and so he came closer to the house and the music, and the singing throbbed in his very ears. He was vastly uneasy, for there was much light round the building. Through every window and doorway it poured out, and the young Suhtai made slow progress, creeping from shrub to shrub, hugging the shadows.

At last he saw a familiar silhouette—and it stood directly beneath a window. Very gladly, Standing Antelope slipped up behind the tall warrior, and rising behind him looked in at the scene whose fascination had turned Thunder Moon to stone.

He saw a large room; and seated at a piano was a girl with glimmering white shoulders, and a tall youth stood beside her to turn her music. And at the farther end of the room sat a gray-haired man and a white-haired woman.

But all the rest were of little meaning to Standing Antelope. He understood in one breath why this long journey had been undertaken. For the face of yonder gray-bearded man was the very face of Thunder Moon himself.

CHAPTER

33

The big man at the window, as though fascinated by the flood of light within the room, remained for a long time staring. Finally he turned, and instantly he grappled with the smaller shadow behind him.

"It is I!" whispered the Cheyenne hastily. "It is Standing Antelope. Take your hand from my throat, Thunder Moon!"

He was free, and the two slipped silently into the adjoining woods where they had left their four horses.

"I, also, have seen," said the boy.

"What?" asked the other.

"I have seen the reason that brought you from the Suhtai and made you travel all these moons into the land of the white men. I have seen his face!"

"You have seen him? Then who is he, Standing Antelope?"

"If he were younger, he would be your brother. But he is too old for that. This is the reason that your skin is pale, Thunder Moon. This is the reason that your ways are not the ways of the Cheyennes. The man who sits in that lodge is your father and you have come this distance to find him!"

There was a rattling of hooves on the hard surface of a bridle path through the woods near by, and suddenly one of the horses neighed loudly. The riders paused and one of them said loudly, in that English tongue that was only beginning to have meaning to the ear of Thunder Moon. "The horses have broken the pasture fence again. George, go in there and have a look and tell me what you find."

"Yes, sir," answered a huskier voice.

Saddle leather creaked as the servant dismounted; and then there was the noise of the man forcing his way through the brush.

Thunder Moon and his companion, however, already were on the backs of their horses; and the pack animals were taken on the lead. Standing Antelope went first, for he had eyes that, among the Suhtai, were said to see in the dark like a cat's. Softly he wove among the tree trunks, but, in spite of all his care, the animals made some noise and there was a sudden hail behind them, "Who's there? Stop!" And then the voice shouted loudly, "Mister Sutton, I seen a man on a horse here. There's something wrong!"

"Thieves, George, by heavens!" cried the other. "Stop them! Fire on them with your pistol!"

"Ride!" said Thunder Moon to the boy ahead of him.

At the same instant a gun cracked behind them and a pistol ball hummed above their heads; a moment later they heard the crashing of brush as "Mister Sutton" jumped his horse in from the roadway.

By this time Standing Antelope had put his pony to full gallop. It was no easy thing to ride with speed through the crowded trees of that copse, but, flattening themselves along the necks of their horses, they swept onward at a smart pace. To the rear they heard shouting voices. Then the noise of one horse in pursuit. But in a few minutes, as they hurdled low fences and plunged across cultivated fields and through strips of woods, the sounds died out.

On a low hilltop they drew rein. They could hear nothing, at first, except the panting of their horses. Then they made out a dim noise of voices from the direction of the great house, and presently there was the cry of dogs.

"I have heard it!" said Thunder Moon in excitement. "The white man hunts with dogs. And now they are coming for us. Ride on, Standing Antelope."

They rode until they came to a sheer slope, at the bottom of which was a considerable stream. It did not stop them; swimming their horses through, they drifted the animals for some time down the shallows on the farther side, then climbed out and up the opposite bank. There they wrung the water from their clothes and listened.

Dawn was beginning as they heard the music of the dog pack swell over the woodland and swing toward them, until the cry of the hounds echoed loud and full over the water.

"If it is your father who lives in the great lodge," said Standing Antelope. "Let us go to him. He will give us shelter in his tribe!"

"How can I tell that he is my father?" replied Thunder Moon. "Two bulls may have the same look, and yet they may come from different herds. I hardly can speak in his tongue; how could I call him my father? Besides," he added more sternly, "I do not come even to a father and ask for help. The men of the Suhtai are free. They do not cringe like coyotes!"

The boy answered a little grimly, "If you are a Suhtai, he is not your father. If he is your father, then you are white and not free. For all white men are slaves. They are slaves to their law at least, as we learned in the wagon train. For their law can whip them, starve them, tie them with rope, or hang them by the neck so that the body and the spirit die together. If you are a Suhtai, you should not be here. If you are a white man and still wish to be free, then go back with me to the Suhtai and live as one of us and remember these people only as one remembers a dream after waking. This is good council, even if I am not a great warrior."

"Peace!" cried Thunder Moon. "You speak with a knife in every word. I shall do the thing that comes to me!"

And so they waited, and heard the noise of the hunt break over the river and stream up to them, through the trees. Then they rode through the copse until they came to a winding roadway. On its firm footing the horses flew. A dust cloud swirled up behind them in the morning light; and Thunder Moon laughed with pleasure.

He did not laugh for long, however. For, looking back down the roadway, he saw that a dozen men were riding hard in pursuit, and gaining fast.

He had no doubt that his stallion could leave the pursuit safely behind. But instantly he doubted the ability of the Indian ponies to withstand such a challenge and over such a course as this.

Even in the distance he could see that the pursuing riders were mounted on animals like his own fine horse. They did not move with a bobbing gallop, like Indian ponies at full speed, but with a long and swinging rhythm they slipped over the ground.

"Full speed!" he called to Standing Antelope.

And the boy, with a shout of determination, gave the whip to his pony and the pack animals.

They did not need two minutes to see how the matter was coming. Tired by a long journey, with many weeks of labor behind them, the ponies were failing fast. Besides, they had behind them horses of some matchless breed, which filled the hearts of the two with wonder and with admiration.

Thunder Moon made up his mind at once.

"There a way turns on the right, Standing Antelope," said he. "When we come to it, take that turning. Take the two spare horses with you, and when the time comes I promise you that all those riders shall follow me."

The boy was too well trained to dispute the word of an older warrior. But he cast one desperate glance behind him at the danger cloud that was rolling up on them so rapidly.

"I shall lead them away," called Thunder Moon, "and then come back to you and find you. Keep to broken country. The short legs of your ponies cannot match the long legs of those horses behind us! What horses they are! But now they shall see what Sailing Hawk can do!"

By a mere pressure of his knees he reduced the pace of the stallion so that he fell well behind; and, turning in the saddle, he drew his rifle from its long holster beneath his right leg.

He balanced it in his hand, and finally twitched the butt of it to his shoulder and fired.

He smiled grimly, seeing two of the pursuers duck low on the necks of their mounts; for he knew that the bullet he sent, though he missed them purposely, must have hummed quite close to their ears.

He waited, then, to see them check their pace, for so any Indian of the plains would have done against such accurate long-range practice as this. But they thrust ahead after him more violently than before, as though they were striving to close the gap before he could load again.

He who could load and fire almost as rapidly as another Suhtai could whip arrows out of the quiver and onto the string!

To prove to the pursuit his skill and the danger of pressing him too closely, he loaded like lightning and discharged a second bullet. This time he took a still closer aim, and again the two leaders winced as the ball cut the air between them. But still they kept on!

It turned the heart of Thunder Moon cold with wonder. These were not the tactics of the plains! And then, in a burst of anger, he prepared for a third shot, which should find a target. Not a man—for these men had not harmed him—but a horse was to be his mark. But when he took within the sights the reaching, lean, beautiful head of one of the horses, his heart failed him. To shoot such an animal was almost worse than to drive a bullet through the body of a rider!

He glanced ahead. Young Standing Antelope, with his two lead horses, had disappeared down the turn to the right. This was the time, then, to show the pursuit what Sailing Hawk could do! Leaning a little in the saddle, Thunder Moon called on the stallion, and there was instant response. From hand canter to racing gallop the big chestnut leaped at a single bound.

For a mile at least that dizzy pace was maintained, and then Thunder Moon looked back to see if the forms of his pursuers were in sight. The result was a shock. They were still in sight, and if they had lost ground, it was a negligible amount! Their speed still seemed to increase and there were more than the original half dozen riders now. Others seemed to have come in from some side road, and fully fifteen horsemen were pressing behind him.

Keen for the hunt, he heard them shout to one another, their voices tingling faintly through the crisp morning air. It dawned suddenly upon Thunder Moon that this might be his last day of riding!

CHAPTER

34

As he steadied the stallion for the race, Thunder Moon tried to understand what was happening. Hitherto, when Indians on the plains challenged him, he had been able to draw away from them with ridiculous ease, in spite of his weight in the saddle. Now his bulk was doubtless greater than that of his pursuers, and doubtless the edge of the stallion's speed had been taken by the long, long journey through all weathers and footings; still it seemed strange that in all the world horses could be found that would stay with him like this.

The hunt was drawing out behind him in a string of riders. So much the speed of Sailing Hawk was accomplishing. But there was no vast distance between the leader and the last of the group.

And they were fresh, terribly fresh, the lot of them. Sailing Hawk ran well, and well he would run until he died. But in the meantime his strength was going. It was not the beginning but the end of a long day for him.

So Thunder Moon decided to try the effect of cross-country work, and sent the stallion at a neighboring fence. Nobly the big chestnut cleared it, and rushed up a gradual slope beyond toward a copse.

Before he disappeared into the woods, Thunder Moon glanced back and saw the first flight of the hunt drive at the same fence. He smiled, waiting to see disaster. But to his amazement, every one of the horses took the obstacle in their stride, not flinging high in the air like Sailing Hawk, but skimming low, with a certain accustomed air, as though jumping were an old matter in their lives. Certainly it was not so with the stallion, accustomed as he was to the open ranges of the plains! And the heart of Thunder Moon sank again.

However, he sent the stallion through the woods, and coming out on the farther side he saw beneath him a stretch of low ground the surface of which was rosy with the morning light.

It was marshland, he could see. Every step of it was glistening with water, and he was forced to turn his horse along the edge of the boggy ground.

A moment later, the hunt poured through the woods. And he heard them shout with triumph, which had a meaning in it, for Sailing Hawk began to flounder heavily. He had gone almost knee-deep in wet soil!

That was the end. Back to the dry ground he had to turn the stallion, and, so turning, he was going straight into the midst of his enemies. There was no need of the rifle here. He thrust it deep in the holster and snatched out the two revolvers that hung at the bow of his saddle. The sway of his body would guide Sailing Hawk as well as reins; each hand was free for a gun, and unless all his long years of training with those difficult weapons had been wasted, there might be a death in every bullet.

Yet it would be hard to fire point-blank upon those men. There was hardly one of them who had not unlimbered rifle or pistol or revolver in turn; but they came toward him now with cheerful shouts, laughing, like careless children at the end of a race for fun.

So he held his fire and waited.

"He's going to fight it out, the nervy devil!" called someone. "Don't shoot, boys. We'll talk some sense into his head, or try to. Jack, you're right. That's one of your horses that he's on!''

They were in evening clothes, all these youths—though such a term had not entered Thunder Moon's vocabulary—and yet they were such born horsemen that they seemed as much at home in the saddle as if they had been in a ballroom. Clean-faced, clear-eyed, eager as hounds, they gathered around Thunder Moon, keeping a proper distance from his poised guns.

In the meantime, the man referred to as " Jack" came to the front and eyed Sailing Hawk with a proprietary air.

"Now, my man," said he, "you're caught, and you're caught barehanded. But you've given us a fine hunt. Only how the devil did you manage to make Cyrus take that jump in such spread-eagle style? Get down, give up your guns, and go along with us. You'll get nothing worse than justice, and maybe something better.''

"By all means better, Jack!" broke in one of the group. "I never knew your Cyrus had such foot. He beat us all!''

"My mare was only warming to her work," protested another.

"But you weigh fifty pounds less than that man-mountain!"

They chaffed one another gaily.

"Get down," repeated Jack. "Get down, man, when I tell you to. You don't think you can stave off the lot of us, do you?''

The English tongue came roughly and slowly to the mind and the lips of Thunder Moon.

"My friend," said he, "you are the chief of this band?"

The other opened his eyes a little more widely.

"Hello!" said he. "This is something special. Am I the chief, he wants to know. Who are you, stranger?''

"I come from the Suhtai," said Thunder Moon gravely.

"Who the devil are the Suhtai? Where do they breed?''

Thunder Moon opened his eyes in turn, for it had not occurred to him that there might be men who did not even know the name of that famous tribe.

"Wherever you come from," said the other, "you've

stolen my horse Cyrus. Get off his back, and after that we'll talk."

"You say a thing that is not true," said Thunder Moon sternly. "This horse is not yours."

"Watch him," said Jack to his companions. "He has a grand face for this sort of work. Doesn't move a muscle while he gets out a thing like that. I don't know my own horses, I suppose?" he continued with a chuckle, facing his captive again.

"If he is your horse," said Thunder Moon, "speak to him, and he will come to you!"

There was a general shout at this.

"That's right, Jack. Talk to him. Make your horse answer back."

"Hold on," replied Jack. "Maybe the fellow's a half-wit. Let's go easy with him."

He controlled his expression and asked more calmly, "If he is your horse, then, he'll come when you call, I suppose?"

"He will, of course," said Thunder Moon.

There was a chorus of whistles.

"Let's see a proof of that!"

One brief syllable of guttural Cheyenne was spoken, and Sailing Hawk dropped to his knees. No trick was more necessary or valuable on the prairies, where a warrior might wish to use his pony as a breastwork in case of a fierce attack. There was a general shout of admiration and amazement from the spectators.

"This *is* something special, Sutton!" said one of the young men.

"Special," said Jack Sutton, "but it doesn't change matters, I suppose no one doubts that that's a Sutton chestnut?"

"He looks the part," said a companion, "but, after all, you can't tell what horses may be in other parts of the world. Certainly that's not a Sutton saddle!"

"We'll talk over the details later on," said Jack Sutton. "Now, my man, just jump off the horse at once, will you? And throw down your guns."

Thunder Moon made no reply.

"Because if you don't," said Sutton, "we'll have to make you, you know!"

"The Suhtai," said Thunder Moon quietly, "die before they give up their guns and their horses. If you fight, some of you must die. In each gun there are six voices."

"Can you believe it?" asked Sutton with growing irritation. "The fool really seems to think he can bluff us out. Now, my friend the horse thief, I'll give you till I count ten before I take you off that horse."

"Friend," answered Thunder Moon, "come one pace nearer to me, and your spirit goes to the Sky People!"

It seemed as though Jack Sutton were about to make that step forward, when one of his friends caught him by the arm and jerked him back.

"The beggar means to do it," he exclaimed, "and by the look of him I think that he'd shoot straight!"

"Are fifteen of us to stand here stopped by one brazen-faced blackguard?" asked young Sutton in a rising fury.

"Come, Jack," said another. "You're the hope of your house. Don't throw yourself away. And, besides, we don't want to murder this nervy rascal. More than that, though, you haven't proved that this is your horse. If he is, he's developed a taste for strange languages! Let me try to handle the case, will you?"

He stepped forward.

"Now, my friend," said he, "you see that we have the numbers. And, of course, we can't afford to be outdone by one man. However, we don't want to keep your back against the wall, and we don't want to murder you. Come with us to the colonel's house and let him hear the story. You make good your claim to the horse and the colonel will never give you a shady deal. You know Colonel Sutton, of course? And of course, you can trust him to do what's right?"

Most of this speech was rather beyond the understanding of Thunder Moon. All that was clear to him was that this speaker was apparently acting as peacemaker; and vaguely he gathered that someone called Colonel Sutton was to be the judge. Colonel was a title like chief among the whites. He knew that also.

So he said, "Let us go to the chief. Some of you may ride beside me to see that I do not run away. But no one rides behind me."

"All fair, all square," said the other. "Satisfactory, Jack?"

"I'd rather have the thing settled here," said Sutton. "Looks as though there weren't enough of us to do justice."

"Enough to do murder, Jack, old fellow; but you spell justice a different way, I take it. Come along, boys, and we'll hear the end of this."

CHAPTER

35

With panting horses, with laughing voices, the party went down the long dusty road.

"That was a run," said one.

"What a burst!"

"Better than fox hunting! The beggar nearly nicked me twice."

"And if he isn't a thief, why did he shoot?"

On the whole, never was there better humor shown by Cheyennes returning from a lucky buffalo hunt than was exhibited now by these fellows who rode so gaily around Thunder Moon. He regarded them not, for his dignity forbade; but all the time, with careful eye, he watched the men who rode on either side of him. Yet, to his surprise, though he had sent two bullets so near them, they treated him with perfect good humor. They rode until they came close behind the great house he had sat down to watch in the middle of the night. Then they turned in, and paused in the arch of the driveway just in front of the mansion.

Since it seemed impossible to get Thunder Moon off his

horse, as a compromise they sent into the building for Colonel Sutton. He came at once, his wife beside him.

The sun was just up, the air was cool and brisk, and the roses that twined up the face of the dwelling, were showering their fragrance on the breeze, while Thunder Moon looked up to the pair standing on the veranda of the house, between the tall, thin, white pillars which framed its entrance. The man, whom they called colonel, was big, powerful of shoulder, grim of expression, and his hair looked silver in that rosy light; by his side, the woman seemed wonderfully thin and delicate. He supported her on his arm, and she seemed frightened, as she looked down on this array of wild young men on their prancing horses. The ball had lasted late at Sutton House, and when the last farewells were said and breakfast finished, they had come to this bright hour of sunrise.

"You'll have to be judge as well as colonel, sir," said young Jack Sutton, standing on the steps beneath his parents. "We've caught a fellow who's a horse thief, as I live. And if that isn't Cyrus that he's riding, anyone may have me!"

The colonel came forward to the edge of the porch.

"The blaze of Cyrus is not so short and wide as that," he said almost instantly. "That isn't one of our horses, Jack. But for all the world, he's one of the strain. That dark chestnut isn't a frequent color. Young man, where did you get that horse?"

The question was clear enough to Thunder Moon, and yet he could make no answer. For a strange new emotion swelled in his throat and stifled him, and he could not take his eyes from the face of the colonel or from that of the little white-haired woman beside him.

"There were two of them in the woods yonder," explained Jack Sutton. "George and I guessed them out and they ran for it. Two men and four horses, and two of the nags with big packs. You'd better look to the silver, mother! This rascal here, when we took after him, opened fire on us. Well, no man shoots to kill unless he has a guilty conscience. That stands for common sense, I suppose."

Thunder Moon was stirred to answer, and he said, "I did not shoot to kill."

"Come, come!" broke in another youngster, though still good humoredly. "Two balls whistled within an inch of my ears. What would you call that?"

"Very interesting," said the colonel. "Very interesting. Come up here, young man, and let me have a talk with you about yourself, and what brought you loitering in the woods, yonder, long after midnight!"

"He won't dismount," broke in Sutton. "Sticks to Cyrus as though he were glued there."

His words were instantly disproved, for Thunder Moon leaped from the back of his horse and, pausing only to sweep his buffalo robe about him, advanced with stately stride toward the porch. Sailing Hawk came close in his rear, and when his master mounted the steps the stallion went up behind him!

There was a little murmur of wonder. The colonel could not help smiling, and his eyes shone. This was a companionship between man and beast such as he loved to see. Not for nothing had he spent the better part of his life and his talents in the rearing of thoroughbreds.

The man from the plains and the colonel stood face to face. There was not a fraction of an inch of difference between them in height; there was no difference in the bulk of their shoulders, which made even the magnificent dimensions of young Jack seem paltry by comparison.

"Now, sir," said the colonel, "let's have an understanding. In the first place, I don't really suspect you. Because a fellow who can train a horse as you've trained that one can't be a sneak thief or a burglar. Where did you get that stallion?"

Thunder Moon, slowly, stretched forth his hand to the west. But his blazing eyes did not leave the face of Sutton for a moment.

"West, eh?" said the colonel. "Well, I didn't know that they raised such animals farther west than my estate. How far west, my friend?"

It was difficult for Thunder Moon to speak, so much was his mind loaded with many reflections.

Then he said, slowly, as he had made his gesture, "Far west—beyond the rivers—in the land of the Cheyennes—"

There was a faint cry—a moan—and the colonel's wife drooped and swayed.

The colonel was swift to turn to her, and his son was still swifter, but the gliding step of Thunder Moon was swiftest of all. He passed between them and caught her in his arms, and held her lightly.

"Now, by heaven!" cried Jack Sutton, vastly alarmed, and reached for his pocket pistol. He did not draw it, however.

For the stranger, standing tall and solemn before them, had altered most wonderfully—a light appeared to break from his eyes and his breast heaved.

"She is not sick," he said quietly. "But the woman is fallen in darkness. She will see again, later on."

"She's overtaxed herself with this infernal ball!" cried the colonel, pale with fear. "Confound me if I'll have dance music in this house again! These waltzes are fit for a madhouse; besides, they're indecent! Martha, do you hear me? Are you better, my dear?"

There was no answer. Mrs. Sutton lay limp, and her head would have fallen back had it not been for the supporting arm of Thunder Moon.

"Give her to me!" exclaimed the colonel.

A dark, gloomy glance was all that answered him, and Thunder Moon stepped past him into the house.

The high rooms soared above him. Beneath his feet was a soft carpeting that mysteriously muffled the fall of his feet—and yet it was not turf! He carried the unconscious woman to a couch, laid her there and kneeled by her side.

"I won't have him touch her," said Jack Sutton furiously. "I won't have it! Why, the common rascal—the scoundrel of a thief!"

"Be still, Jack," said his father. "Don't be ridiculous. He treats her as though she were precious. There's something not common about this man."

"Hello!" cried Jack. "What's in that flask? Are we going to have her poisoned? What's in that leather pouch?"

Thunder Moon turned his head toward the younger man and answered, "Water—brother!"

There was something in the intonation of his voice, and something in the dark glance of his eyes that made Jack Sutton catch his breath and look to his father as though for advice.

At the taste of the cold water, the colonel's wife stirred, moaned a little, opened her eyes, and stared wildly up to the stern, dark face above her.

"Randolf!" breathed Mrs. Sutton.

At that, the colonel moved between her and Thunder Moon.

"What is it?" he asked. "What is it, Martha? Did something upset you? What's wrong?"

"I can't think! I don't dare think! I'm going mad, Randolf!"

"Ruth," said Jack, to a girl who now ran into the room, "see what you can do. Something's wrong with mother—and I think it's that rascally horse thief fellow who's done it!"

"Who?" cried the girl.

She turned and saw Thunder Moon, wrapped again in his robe, his arms folded beneath it, his bowed head turned toward the woman on the couch.

"Ah!" gasped Ruth Sutton, and she clung close to her brother.

"Good Lord!" exclaimed Jack, irritated rather than sympathetic. "He's not a ghost. He's a man, you know. He's not a ghost!"

"Are you sure?" stammered Ruth. "Are you sure that he's not a ghost?"

Jack Sutton had stood enough. He strode up to Thunder Moon.

"Sir," said he, "whatever happens, I'm afraid that you're a scoundrel. But before you're one minute older, I'll have your name, and who you are, and where you've come from, and all the rest of it!"

"Brother," said the tall man, and again there was a strange intonation of the word, "on the plains in the West the Suhtai know me, and they have given me a name."

"Suhtai again. And who the devil are the Suhtai?"

"Are you better, Martha?" asked the colonel. "Steady,

now. Has this fellow upset you at all? Is it he? I know the Suhtai. And so do some of our troopers, worse luck. They're a tribe of the Cheyennes, Jack.''

"God bless me!" cried Jack, and moved a pace away. "I thought there was something odd about him. Are you an Indian, then?''

"What I am," said Thunder Moon, raising his head, "I cannot tell. And as for my name, I have come a great journey; I have traveled for more than one moon, to come at last to this place to learn what my name might be.''

"Why, the fellow has no wits, Indian or white," said Jack Sutton. "He says that he's come here to find out what his name may be!''

"I knew it!" cried the colonel's wife.

"I knew it! I knew it!" cried Ruth, pointing with a rigid arm.

Jack Sutton took his sister by both arms.

"I almost think there's some foolish plot between you and mother," he said. "I really almost think there is. What the devil is it that you and she know that has to do with this fellow, that neither of you have ever seen before?''

"Oh, you're blind! You're utterly blind!" cried Ruth. "Both of you are blind! Look at him again!''

"I see him. What of it? What of it?''

"Dad," Ruth exclaimed, running to her father and clinging to his arm.

"Let me alone. Your mother looks very ill, Ruth.''

"She's not—joy doesn't bring harm. Dad, won't you look at him? Won't you see?''

"See what, child? Damn it, Ruth, what's in your mind? What is this mystery?''

"Don't you understand? He says that he's come back here to find his name—''

"That's nonsense!''

"But it isn't! I know what his name is!''

"The devil you do! What is it, then?''

"It's William Sutton, and he's your own son. Don't you see? He's come back! He's come back to you!''